SAYONARA BABY

AN AUSTRALIAN FUGUE NOVEL

Also by Ruth Skilbeck

Australian Fugue series novels
The Antipode Room with images
Sayonara Baby (previously published as a stand-alone with the title *Cafe Life in the Antipodes*)

Related works
Missing (abridged edition of Australian Fugue)
Sayonara Baby-Fragments of Memory Images photographic art images and brief excerpts from Australian Fugue novels

Musico-literary studies
The Writer's Fugue: Musicalization, Trauma and Subjectivity in the Literature of Modernity

Anthology and Journal
Escape Artists Anthology - editor
Arts Features International - editor-in-chief

RUTH SKILBECK
SAYONARA BABY

AN AUSTRALIAN FUGUE NOVEL

BORDERSTREAM BOOKS

This story is a work of fiction. Names, characters, places, and incidents are the product of the author's imagination or are used fictitiously. Textual references to art, film, books, artists, and events, are included to create background, and any perceived resemblance to actual persons, events or locales is unintended and coincidental.

Contents

Prelude   9

Samuel and the Lone Deranger   11

Medusa   82

Heatwave   93

Words   105

Japan   125

Sayonara, Baby   130

Music   145

Reggie's Rooms   171

The Missing Typewriter   200

Rocky Horror Show   214

Departure   230

Slugs   237

Notes and Acknowledgement   240

Author's Note   241

Cross the Rubicon
and you will see
a darker entrance
to the sea

a funfair waits
on the other side
you don't see the horror
till you go on the ride

a creepy clown c
repeats d to infinity
you're on the way
when you say 'gee'

Prelude

1975-1976

I had never had a cappuccino before I left Northern Ireland. But since arriving in Australia drinking this kind of coffee in cafés had become a major part of my life here, it was a ritual that kept me sane.

It had been that way ever since I arrived in Canberra with Dad, and had to stay with him alone in the flat in University House until the government allocated family house became available and we moved to the outer reaches of the (un)known universe. I had supped on delicacies in Japan on the way to my new life down under, but it was not green tea or sake that had stamped an impression indelibly in my soul. The healing elixir had been cappuccino—not a drink one associates with Japan; my first ever, in an outdoor café next to a cable car in a scenic mountain range east of Kyoto, where Dad and I had made a surprising (to me) encounter with Dad's work friend, the glamorous New Yorker Francesca Bellinka, the first person I'd met who always dressed in black. She was a favourite family friend of mine. She was at the conference too, and she popped up one afternoon for a sightseeing excursion. Before we went on the cable car across a ravine, we had refreshments.

She perused the menu, then said in a purring tone, "Well I know we're in Japan but I've never liked green tea. I'm going to have a cappuccino, how about you Roxy"?

She looked at me with a smile.

"What's that?"

She laughed. "You're joking, right?"

"No! I'm not!" It was indeed true. The menu in the local caff in Ballyhope had offered nothing more exotic than teabag tea and instant coffee.

"Marcus!" she said in a mock chastising tone. "How could you have not introduced her to cappuccino?" As if it were a failing in my upbringing, or education.

"What is it?"

"It's coffee made from real coffee beans, topped with fluffed up milk sprinkled with chocolate. You'll love it!"

She was right.

When we arrived in Canberra, I found cafés that made cappuccino, which were run by Italian or Greek people, families, I discovered as I went to all of them, comparing their cappuccino in Civic, the centre of the city. Every day when Dad was at work, I would walk into the city centre which was as little like such a thing as I could ever have imagined. I would shop for food, then have a cappuccino, "with lots of froth". Soon I discovered the library, and would go there first when I reached the centre. I'd take my borrowed books by Böll, or Camus, or Sartre, or Kafka, to a café and read for hours, in between scrawling lines of thoughts in my notebooks.

It was a habit that continued.

Samuel and the Lone Deranger

31 December 1980–November 1981

1

I arrived in Adelaide with Sam on his 1000 cc motorbike. Samuel and I were supposed to have split up weeks before but it hadn't quite worked out. It seemed we were still spending all of our time together. As I'd packed up my things in the garage by the lake where I lived preparing to set off to start university alone he'd insisted on taking me: "Just to see you settled in." I privately thought that I was quite capable of settling in all by myself but there seemed little point in arguing. We'd been together for four years, and had travelled far on the outback and back roads on his bike, we might as well part on good terms. And have one last long roadtrip.

It was a two-day ride of over a thousand kilometres taking the interior highways. Setting off mid-afternoon, five hours straight on the bike, and we crossed the Hay Plains at night. The motorbike was the fastest and almost the only vehicle on the road; we sped for hours overtaking the few cars and trucks we passed along the mind-bendingly straight line. A bright silver full moon shone down, on either side the highway long fields of tall wheat appeared to ripple in luminous waves, with a cold distant radiance the moon lit the way.

Samuel and I had been to Adelaide the year before on our trip around Australia. We'd stayed with an inner-city philanthropist Samuel met in a shop in North Adelaide. Tony gave shelter to motorbikers in his cottage from pure generosity of spirit, asking for nothing in return. We'd ridden into town from the desert, covered in red bulldust—as local people call the soft red sandy earth—and dehydrated. He'd offered us his front room where we'd stayed for a week. Samuel was good at making these arrangements with people. He was good looking and charismatic. With the motorbike with its panniers parked nearby, as he browsed the community noticeboards in alternative wholefood stores, nibbling high-energy bars—in his black leathers, contrasting with his long curly-haired ponytail, big wide smile, backpack, me behind him—something physically magnetic about Sam attracted locals and inspired trust. They came up and talked; offered to let us sleep in their barns, outhouses, and houses.

When we arrived in Adelaide late in the afternoon, Sam and I went straight to Tony's. We hadn't been in touch with Tony for over a year but he welcomed us in like old friends.

Two weeks later

The next day in the local paper I saw a room to rent in a house in Norwood, in eastern Adelaide, rang the number, and spoke to the man who answered who said he was called Frank. He sounded okay. I said I was in Adelaide to start university; he said he had gone to the university and had been president of the Student Unity Progress Group. "That sounds alright," said Samuel; we rode over to look at it that evening.

A short haired, stocky man in a leather jacket opened the door; he was about the same height as me. He sized us up.

"What are you riding?" he demanded, warily.

Sam said the make. It was often the first question people asked. In the world of bikes on the road it seemed what make you rode defined what kind of person you were, what culture you were part of. It was known as a high speed touring bike.

"Come in."

We walked through the door holding our helmets.

"Where're you from?"

"Canberra," we chorused.

"Roxy's come here to go to university."

"Been to Adelaide before?"

"Yes. Just rode through, last year when we were travelling."

"Well this is the room," he gestured through an open door. We walked in and looked around at a large room with pieces of coconut matting on the floor, a bay window, and fireplace.

"Looks good," I said politely.

"I was president of the Student Unity Progress Association, when I was there." Frank repeated what he'd told me on the phone."

"Oh yeah," said Sam. "When was that?"

"Few years ago."

"What are you doing now?"

"Few things. Didn't finish uni," he said evasively. His tone was defensive. "I'll show you round."

He showed us the bathroom, living room, and kitchen in a converted veranda at the back.

"Hmm, yeah, looks good," we made polite noises.

"Meet Cory. He's not well. Cory, you awake?"

"Come in," a high-pitched voice said, after Frank pushed open the bedroom door.

Cory was a frail-looking youth with delicate features and a

sweet smile. No older than me.

"Hi," he said.

"Hi Cory," Sam said.

"Hi," I smiled at him.

"You know," said Frank in the assertive tone of a raconteur. "Adelaide is not like other cities in Australia. It's the only city that wasn't founded by convicts. It's middle class and genteel. Adelaide people take pride in that."

"Oh." "Ah." We had heard this before.

"But you know, there are very strange crimes in Adelaide."

"Yeah?" Sam said.

"Are there?" I added.

"Yes," Frank said warming to his narrative. He glanced over our shoulders at Cory in bed in their bedroom.

"There are. For a few years, there have been lots of murders, and abductions, a couple, a man high up in the establishment and a younger guy who he was in love with were going out on drives in his car. They would pick up women, and hitchhikers, offer them a lift, the younger guy would rape them while the older one watched then they would murder them."

"God."

"Ugh," said Sam.

"Yeah. We know people who knew one of them; they were part of the gay scene. We know about it."

Sam said, as if it called for a reciprocal anecdote: "When we were travelling last year we were stopped by police, weren't we Roxy, warning us, 'cause we were riding the same bike as that couple who were stabbed to death in their tent as they slept in the camp-site outside Tennant Creek."

"Yeah?"

"They were riding the same make and model bike. Travelling the exact same route we were."

"The cops always said to us to be careful. They were travelling with a guy on a bike that was the same make as the guy's we were travelling with, too."

"Yeah, we met him on the road, and in places we stayed, we kept bumping into him, we were travelling the same way, so sometimes we rode and stayed at places together," I added.

It was a disturbing coincidence. My mother had been very worried and I had to ring her once a week to let her know that we were okay.

"It was pretty freaky."

Frank added, "There are other things going on here, strange crimes. Be careful," he added looking at me.

"How long would you be here?" He asked Sam, again.

"A few days, a week or so." Sam looked at me.

"That should be okay. The room's just for one," said Frank.

We moved in and I arranged things. I put the backpacks in a wardrobe. Samuel took me to the university on the bike and I enrolled.

A couple of evenings later when Frank came in his manner seemed aggressive. I could feel the charged currents of the air as he walked in. Cory was still in bed. Samuel had gone out to do something about bike repairs. I was in the kitchen, making a cup of tea.

Frank strode in carrying a plastic shopping bag. "I'm going to the gym. Taking steroids. Gonna build myself up again."

Ignoring pleasantries, dramatically, he thrust his arm into his plastic bag, grabbed and roughly shook something inside, and with a flourish pulled out of the bag—a large piece of raw meat. He held it aloft then threw it onto a chopping board.

He looked at me, directly acknowledging my presence for the first time since walking into the kitchen.

He reached into a cupboard, took out a jar, and brandished it in front of me. "Meet the household pet."

Motionless on a blade of grass was a large black spider. A patch of red adorned its shiny back.

"She's called Blanche! *Latrodectus hasseltii*. Female! She's a cousin of the black widow but far more dangerous. If she bites you her venom could kill you within half an hour. Found her in the back yard."

I didn't say a word in reply.

Frank picked up a large marble pestle.

"How's it going at uni?"

"Okay. This week I'm just enrolling early."

"What subjects are you taking?

"Philosophy and English and Drama," I said politely but I felt as if it were a little hard to breathe in this room.

"I took." He lifted the pestle high.

"Philosophy!" The man barked, slamming the blunt object onto the hunk of bloody meat.

He raised the pestle. "Politics!" Slam. He beat the oozing cut of organ or whatever it was.

He raised the pestle. "Economics!!" Splat. He pounded the meat as he snarled the word as if he were in an aggressive competition. The stench of death filled the room; the foul innards glistened beneath the electric light.

"When's your boyfriend leaving? The room is just for one."

I felt uncomfortable. Surely it would be impolite to just leave the kitchen. I felt like I did when I was hitchhiking, in a car, and had to humour the driver to keep myself as safe as possible. I pretended not to notice the aggressive energy crackling in the air, ratcheting up each time he beat the piece of dead creature with the pestle.

"At the gym they were telling me about some things."

I stared at the redback spider in its jar. I felt my throat dry. I had a feeling like earth in my mouth.

"I knew the guys who were murdering those women. They were getting a kick out of it. You know you have to be careful," he said in a warning tone.

He roughly opened a drawer, took out a knife, and violently slashed a line across the slice of fresh carcass.

"Lots of men get a kick out of harming women, murder."

"Well, must get on! Things to do!" I tried to sound unperturbed by what he was saying and doing. I didn't want him to know he was making me (very) uneasy.

He did not reply to my brave *bon mot*.

I took my cup of tea, backing out of the kitchen, quickly.

I hurried into my room, past Frank and Cory's closed door.

There was no lock on the door of my room.

I stood in the room, anxiously awaiting Samuel's return.

Half an hour passed, and then I heard the familiar puttering sound of Sam's bike. I hurried to the front door before he rang the bell as he did not have a key.

In a whisper I told Sam what had happened in the kitchen. "Really??" he said. "A redback?"

"Yep." I wanted to say that I was feeling very uncomfortable here. But it was probably obvious.

On Saturday, five days after I'd moved in, all the occupants were in the house. Frank was not at work or whatever it was he did. He had not said. Cory was still ill in bed. Samuel was wearing his leather jacket and jeans. Fixing something on the bike in the front garden. On the night we looked at the place, Sam had been wearing a raw wool jumper that had the effect of making his shoulders and chest look a lot smaller than they were. About mid morning he came into my room where I was reading. He took off his jacket and jeans.

"It's hot outside," he said, smiling at me. He went back out wearing a tee-shirt and shorts.

Frank strode into the kitchen as we were clearing up after an early lunch.

He walked past Sam, who was drying a plate.

He took out a piece of dead meat from a white plastic bag and put it in the fridge.

When Samuel left the kitchen Frank said, "He's bigger than I thought." His tone was threatening. I struggled to catch his meaning. The sense of unease that I had felt since I moved in suddenly increased.

Samuel walked back into the kitchen and poured himself a glass of water from the tap.

"Work out?" Frank said with hostility. His tone was intimidating, as if Sam and I had done something very wrong, as if we had deliberately concealed Samuel's size.

"Just one hundred push-ups a day, mate."

Frank broke two eggs slowly. He poured the innards out in a bowl and attacked what he was making with an eggbeater.

"Come into the garden later and I'll show you the compost heap I'm making." Frank looked at Samuel.

"Okay," Sam replied. "I've almost finished fixing the bike."

Samuel walked outside. I nonchalantly strolled back to the not-reassuringly unlocked refuge of my room.

I was reading at the table by my window, which had a view of a tall hedge bordering the street.

Samuel was in the garden still repairing the bike, or talking about gardening with Frank. Or, that's what I thought. Then I saw Frank walking out the gate, onto the street, which I could see from where I was sitting.

I could hear Samuel's voice out in the hallway, his soft quiet tenor, that I felt in my body as much as heard. He was talking to Cory in bed. Then he pushed open the door in a hurry.

"Roxy. Quick! Pack up all your things, everything. We've got to leave before Frank gets back! Cory says he'll be about an hour."

He didn't need to say anything more.

We shared an instinctive telepathic sense of danger that had protected us through our travels through the deserts when we had scarce supplies, only a cardboard box balanced on my knee with a few crispbread and a cabbage or whatever greens we'd be lucky to find in roadhouse shops on the thousands of kilometre dirt tracks of unsealed roads. Marked as places, towns on the maps, they were no more than a couple of petrol pumps and a house, which might have a bar and a shop filled with cans of meat. There might be mass produced meat snacks such as beefo rolls which were frozen, then deep fried. As we were both vegetarian, we had very little to eat for days on end.

One time we pulled into one of these places. There was an Aboriginal camp on the other side of the track, in the desert scrub. Outside the pub, a long line of local people stood in the heat. We got off the bike. Samuel lifted up the handle of the petrol pump and held it in the tank. We looked at the pub. All across the front were hand-painted messages.

NO BOONGS!
NO ABOS ALLOWED. COONS OUTSIDE
BLACK C***S BANNED
I walked around to the side of the pub to see what people were queuing up for. There was a window counter from which alcohol was being sold, under hate words:
BOONGS SERVO
The prices were written in aggressive-looking letters:
BEER $30 A STUBBY. PORT $90 BOTTLE
That was at least ten times the usual amount.
"Is that how much they charge?" I asked a man in a cowboy hat. I gestured at the signs.
"And they won't let you inside? And those disgusting signs?"
"Yeah… that's right." He looked at me then looked down. Several people looked at me, and then quickly looked away.
"It's disgusting," I said as Samuel walked up.
We'd walked resolutely, and with anger. Towards the pub, pushed open the saloon door.
A few men wearing shorts and checked flannel shirts were sitting around inside, at the bar, and in a saloon. They looked up as we walked in.
"G'day mate," the bar tender said. "Whaddaya havin'?"
"Bin ridin' far"?
"Whaddaya ridin' mate?"
The men were always affable to Samuel, wherever we went. But this time he would not have the usual friendly chat.
"I'll just have a glass of water, thanks."
"Two." I added.
We drank deeply the tap water, much better than the bore water which we'd been drinking and had to drink on the road, and which was so full of sediments, salts and minerals I had to

throw it down my throat to try to avoid my taste buds.

We placed down empty glasses. I felt the surge of adrenalin, and hard controlled contempt.

"We think you're disgusting, mate," said Samuel.

"Who the hell do you think you are? You charge the Aboriginal people ten times more for alcohol, and won't let them inside, it's disgraceful!"

"What do you think gives you any right to treat Aboriginal people like that?" Samuel jeered.

"It's their country!!" I yelled.

We stormed out. We fastened helmet straps under chins, pulled on gauntlet gloves; jumped on the bike. Samuel kicked down on the kick-starter, opened up the accelerator and we roared out of there in a great cloud of red dust.

Although we had our differences, these were over personal matters; this was one of the times that Samuel and I were fully united in thought and action.

Now we were leaving this house. But quietly and surreptitiously, and again united.

These thoughts were swirling around my mind as I packed up the panniers.

"Roxy," he whispered urgently. "If Frank comes back *don't* say you're moving out. I've told Cory we're going to the beach for the afternoon."

We had packed almost all our belongings in the panniers that Samuel had attached to the bike, and the backpack, which was outside. I was filling my khaki army surplus shoulder bag with books that had not fitted, along with my notebook and water bottle.

"Roxy," Sam hurried back into the room. "Wait outside for me. I'm just going to say goodbye to Cory."

I walked out, surprised that he wanted to say goodbye. Time passed. He was taking ages. What was he doing in there?

More time passed. I heard a car parking; a car door closing, behind the hedge. Then Frank came into view.

He pushed open the garden gate. Glanced at the bike with a look of menace. The front door was open. He hurried inside.

Why was Samuel taking so long? I fretted.

I waited, and waited, fighting down rising fear.

Eventually he walked out.

"We're going." His face was pale; features solidified in an inscrutable mask. I could tell he was unusually shaken.

We put on our crash helmets. He straddled "the monster," manoeuvred the bike around and I sat behind him. He kicked down, opened up the accelerator.

We roared out of that garden that I was starting to think I would be stuck in forever.

After we had been on the road riding through the suburbs for a while, we pulled into a service station. *My Sharona* blasted out from a car at the petrol pumps. The familiar kitschy radio tune made me feel a little more at ease. All seemed relatively normal here.

"I'm glad we're away from there, there was something really off about that place." I acted cheerful, as if trying to restore a lost mood.

"Yeah."

"That guy was creepy."

"It was getting much worse." Sam's tone was terse. I waited but he said no more.

"What shall we do?"

"Go back to Tony's."

"Okay."

We went back to Tony's. We told him what had happened.

"Stay here as long as you like," he said. That evening after dinner we were in the kitchen, finishing the washing up. Tony walked in and became loquacious:

"You know, it's a thing about Adelaide. It's the only city in Australia that wasn't settled by convicts. People take pride in it. It's known as the City of Churches. But instead there's a different kind of crime that happens here. People disappear. There have been murders of women thought to be hitchhikers. An older man and a younger guy were picking up women, raping and murdering them. There are white collar crimes that don't happen anywhere else in Australia. It's still happening—right now."

Samuel and I glanced at each other.

"We've heard that," said Sam. I didn't say anything. Neither of us wanted to prolong this conversation.

Sam looked at the wall clock. "Geez, it's nine thirty. Well I guess it's time to hit the hay."

* * *

A month or so later
The next day, on a local health-food store Community Board, I saw a hand-written notice:

Broad-minded person (preferably student)
wanted to share 3-bedroom house with three First
Year fine art students and cat.
One street from beach.
88 Rubicon Road, Glenelg.

There was a phone number. I rang and spoke to a male voice introducing himself as "Fraser." We rode over that evening to Rubicon Road. The house was a white brick bungalow, in a road one street from the beach, beyond a gutter full of silver sand. I went first down the concrete path to the side entrance porch, Samuel following close behind. I rang the bell.

A tall smiling guy, good-looking, with short dark hair and floppy fringe, opened the door straight away.

"Hi," I said, "I've come a—"

"Come in, come in," the guy said. "The others are in the living room. Come this way!"

We followed him in single file down a long unlit hallway, carpeted with coconut matting.

Two girls jumped up as we walked into the living room.

"I'm Fraser, I'm the one whose name is on the lease," said the tall, gangling guy. He extended his arm. I shook his hand.

"Pleased to meet you!"

"I'm Lily," a red-haired girl holding a large white cat, said.

"And this is Giles." She held up her cat, smiling, narrowing her eyes. I looked at her in surprise. Not only did she have the same name and hair colour, she looked a little like Lily, my sister.

"And this is my girlfriend, Margarita," Fraser said. Now I did a double take.

"This is such a coincidence!" I said. "My sister is called Lily and she has red hair; and my best friend is called Margarita and she has black hair. You're both about the same height as they are too!"

Everyone laughed.

"Some call me Margie, some call me Rita. Most people call me—Margarita!"

"You can call me what you like so long as you don't call me late for lunch! Boom Boom!" joked Fraser.

We all groaned.

"What star signs are you?" I asked.

"Scorpio," said Lily.

"Taurus!" Margarita replied.

"So are they, each of them!" I groaned again. "This is too much!"

"What are you?" asked Margarita.

"Cancer."

"So is one of my sisters! What day's your birthday?"

"The eighth of July."

"Hers is the ninth of July!"

"Life is full of coincidences!" said Sam, winking at Fraser.

"We thought I'd found a place," I ventured. "We moved in, but it wasn't okay."

"No?" said Fraser.

"NO." They all looked at me. I tried to make light of it. "It was actually really weird, pretty scary."

They kept looking at me.

"Guy with a huge redback spider for a pet, who was getting really aggressive."

"He'd started taking steroids, he kept talking about women being murdered. It was getting uncomfortable," Sam added.

"Gee." Margarita exclaimed.

"You'll be safe here," said Lily.

"It's been in the news a lot, you've probably heard about it, seen it on TV, the young guys, hitchhikers?" said Fraser. "As well as that case that's been in the papers, of the homosexual couple the older man and his boyfriend who were murdering women hitchhikers. There's another one coming to trial soon, you might have heard of it."

"We never watch TV, or read the papers, or listen to radio," said Sam.

"Really?" said Fraser, looking startled.

"I haven't watched TV once since I moved to Australia four years ago, and we never read the papers, or listen to the radio."

"Why not?" Margarita asked.

"The media is addictive. Moulds how people think. It's fake news, it's mental pollution, social conditioning" said Samuel.

"Better off without it—for writing. It's too noisy." I added.

"Where did you live before in England?" Margarita asked.

"I lived in Northern Ireland."

"Roxy's a writer," Samuel said. "She's had poems and short stories published."

"There's no TV here!" said Lily.

"You can get more work done, if you cut yourself off from the world," said Margarita.

I was surprised, and relieved and pleased that they were taking what I was saying seriously and agreeing with it. After the years on the bike on the road I was not used to socialising with people who were artists and writers.

"Move in tonight if you like," Fraser added.

* * *

Four days later

I moved in next day. Samuel put the panniers and helmets in the corner of my room, saying he'd only stay a couple of days. The next day, he bought me a desk from a second-hand shop. Spending money—for him that was quite an event. When I got home from my first day at the University, I found that he'd arranged my painting things neatly on its surface.

"Thanks Samuel, that's great." Of course I was incapable of organizing my own work surfaces.

Fraser was the newly appointed Art School social secretary, and he organized. The next night there was a Freshers' party at the house. By 8 p.m. the place was packed with people who'd just met, shouting, talking, and pouring drinks in the kitchen, a lot of highly excited first year art students in the dark living-room bopping away to Daddy Cool. Someone put on *Rock Lobster* by the B-52s; *Anarchy in the UK,* the Sex Pistols. I stood in the doorway, wondering if I should dance. There was someone who looked rather different dancing.

He looked older, and more self-assured. Dressed in black, with short spiky red hair. He was dancing alone in the centre of the room. Swigging wine from a plastic cup, laughing for no apparent reason. On his black tee-shirt were the words *The Lone Deranger* in dripping letters the colour of blood.

Fraser touched my elbow, staring at the dancer. "Look."

"That," he said dramatically, pointing discreetly and rolling his eyes. "That is Raymond Furnett. One of the leather-jacket boys... A group of fourth-year destructive... idiots... conceptual artists... a public disturbance... throwing their weight around, and they call it Art."

I couldn't hear all he was saying. I glanced at the dancer with increased interest. He didn't glance back.

Lily ran in, eyes glowing, holding a stick of pink fairy-floss.

"We've just been on the Big Wheel and the dodgems," she shouted.

"You get such a view when it's right at the top, then going down, it's so thrilling!"

Later, at the front door, I almost fell over the dancer sitting on the doorstep with Lily. Wearing a slinky silver skirt and high-heeled slides; three years younger than me, seventeen. What was he doing talking to her?

"Hey Roxy!" she said, looking up at me, her bright blue mascara shining. "This is Raymond Furnett, he's in fourth year. Raymond, this is Roxy. She lives in the house too. She's at university. She's from Sydney. She's here with her boyfriend. He's the one with the motorbike…"

"G'day," said Raymond, looking at me.

"Hi," I said, looking back at him.

Yowch!! A physical sensation, like an electric shock, zapped through my nervous system; I took one step back.

"Ray's just asked me if I'll go to the cinema with him," Lily said, laughing.

"Isn't that so sweetly romantic and old-fashioned?"

"Mm mmm…" I laughed merrily, raising my left eyebrow.

"How delightful. An old fashioned boy…"

I walked around the party restlessly for an hour or so. The charge I got when I was introduced to Raymond Furnett had affected me. It had opened up a new hunger, for what I did not know. I felt an overpowering Desire for experiences that would open up possibilities, realms of being and becoming, new knowledge, change my life; I wanted to meet different people, have new adventures that would jolt perception, open unknown ways of seeing, being and feeling.

That's why I had come here to study Arts. Two years after I'd finished school; I'd travelled Australia with Samuel. I wanted to find out—about the world, myself and other people.

I walked through the groups of fresher students, drinking and chatting in the living room, with its coconut matting and turquoise-blue ceiling, congregating in the kitchen, splashing wine, talking loudly. I glanced at the glossy poster promoting sweet white Moselle wine that Fraser had stuck onto the wall, next to his side of the food cupboard. It was all so tame.

I wanted to keep on moving. I walked out the front door, down the path onto the pavement. On the far side of Rubicon Road was a fairground, just over from it, was the beach and the Bay. From the window of my new bedroom, I could see the spokes and upper rim of the Big Wheel against the sky. I'd heard it creaking in the wind as I fell asleep at night, Samuel beside me on the double mattress on the floor. The funfair was closed now.

I walked down the sandy street towards the silent rides. Living next to a fairground had undoubted appeal. As a child, visiting a funfair had been a pinnacle experience. Abandoning oneself to excesses of sensation on the rides tested the nerves, obliterating decorum in the liberating physical thrill of release. A turn on the roller coaster was a journey through anticipation, screaming terror, exhilaration, and relief. All the way, from seduction to desire to full-on climax of terror, the funfair promised, and delivered experiences of sensation unlike any other public events I'd experienced, and I could never quite believe it was real. Like the circus, or the pantomime, or ballet performances at the Old Vic, funfairs had the aura of magic that separated them from everyday reality. Every year, when I was a kid in England, we went to Weston-Super-Mare for my birthday; at the end of the party, I held my breath in anticipation of the promised climax; after our ritual trek across the mud flats to try to find the sea, the consumption of party food on the beach, my friends and I raced each other all the way to the funfair at the end of the pier. To abandon our young selves, in a frenzy of screaming and shrieking as loudly as possible on the dodgems, and further gorge ourselves with sticky fairy-floss and ice creams. Best of all, when I was older and our family moved to County Antrim, Northern Ireland, was the fairground Big Dipper at Portrush, this was a guaranteed ticket to adrenalin-overloading terror, exhilaration of survival. So long as you had the guts to go on it, the experience never failed to exceed expectations. Why is it that the rest of life never matches such peak physical experiences, I thought. I read a sign that said the funfair closed at 9 p.m. on Fridays and Saturdays in summer; this had been the last late night, soon would come the silence and shadows of out-of-season melancholia.

I walked past the fairground and down towards the famous Glenelg Pier and the esplanade, where groups of Aboriginal people gathered to socialize on the grass outside the Regal Hotel. A couple of days ago I took up their invitation, sat down and shared a drink with them. (Or rather, I pretended to swig from the bottle they passed around. I didn't let my lips touch the bottle neck—so what did that make me? A wimp, a poseur, or a hopeless phoney?) Now there were a couple of people around, in the distance, strolling along the esplanade. I kept walking fast over the grass, down a flight of stone steps and onto the pale silver beach.

I lay on my back on the sand, staring up at the stars. It was a clear night. The dark sky glittered with countless dots and speckles of light. At first I could only make out the main constellations that I recognized, the Southern Cross, big Orion, little Orion, also known as Big and Little Saucepan. Venus, which was both the evening and morning star, different names for each time of day it was viewed, was it correct to call it the 'same' star? As my eyes adjusted to the night I detected more swirling clouds and traces of light in the blackness. I knew that what I could see was a paradox of time and space. The traces of cloudy light were nothing but traces: memories, ghosts of galaxies—that did not exist in time now but had existed millions of light years ago. So what was I looking up into; what was I seeing?

It was extraordinary, I thought. Looking up into the clear night sky, in Australia, I was travelling through Time. It was like looking up into the memory of a whisper of the voice of 'God', Goddess, or creator beyond all notions of names, a force comprehensible to me, here on earth; swirling the pot of the great cauldron of matter or non-matter called 'space'... a concept of galaxies beyond galaxies beyond everything and nothing, too vast to comprehend...

I had a giddy feeling as if the night was opening up to me a pathway, showing me a secret... I remembered from what I had found out in chemistry at school, that carbon, one of the basic elements of DNA, comes from stars. If that was right, that meant part of my body and mind might be made of an exploded star... maybe I was looking up at its ghost, its memory, right now....and it was telling me something as I lay on the sand, staring up into the night.

Be brave and strong...

Follow your dreams...

I had come to Adelaide to go to university, to follow my destiny. Here, lying on this beach, gazing up into millions of undiscovered galaxies, I thought: anything is possible.

Everything that happens will be all right...

A few days later Raymond moved into Lily's room. I saw him in the daytime. Sometimes I heard them at night through the thin wall that separated our rooms. Making love and talking.

One day Fraser said to Lily, "You're only seventeen". To our amusement, he looked scandalized.

"So?" she said, laughing. "What about you and Margarita? And she's married."

Margarita who was older than us, twenty-four, had told us she'd left her husband to go to Art School. She and Fraser met in Orientation Week, and decided to move in together.

Lily and Raymond appeared to have developed an enviable closeness, a cool intimacy. In comparison, it felt like my relationship with my teetotalling bike-riding boyfriend—which was supposed to be over—had become a straitjacket of personal penance and bizarre, hypocritical crime. Every day, there were routines he had to follow with rigid precision. One-hundred-push-ups. And the stealing of at least one conveniently sized food-item from the small supermarket across the road from the house: blocks of cheese, packets of dried fruit and nuts, anything handy, of a suitable size, that he could conceal down the front of his shorts, or in his motorbike helmet. Samuel was the only person I knew of with a large inheritance. He was also the only one I knew who harboured an urge to steal. Infuriatingly to me, it had become a matter of his personal pride to never spend a cent unless it was impossible not to.

I kept thinking about the time his mother visited him, a couple of years ago, about his twenty-first birthday. She came to the share-house in Kingston, our house, but, instead of his mother coming into the house to talk, Samuel had sat alone with her in her car on the road outside for about an hour. When he returned, his manner towards me had noticeably changed. It was subtle. But I sensed an aloofness and distance. He didn't face me as he spoke to me. He told me that his mother had been telling him things he needed to know. *She said I have to be careful. She said: When you have money,* he said the words carefully, *you can never be certain what people really think of you or why they want to be friends with you. And you can never tell how people you know will change when you do come into money. Even close friends. She was surprised how even good friends of her own changed when she came into her inheritance.* She told him these were truths he had to know.

This was all in preparation for the Big Event. When he would come into his inheritance at the age of twenty-one. Samuel's father had committed suicide when Samuel and his twin brother were only thirteen. Samuel had said to me that his father had never recovered from after-affects of the war, and the Holocaust in Germany, which his wealthy father's family had fled, to avoid being exterminated in death-camps. When Samuel's mother left his father, for the principal of her boys' school, Samuel's father killed himself. He had not said any more detail than that. Samuel confided that his father had left them money, and a terrace house in Sydney each that they would inherit, that had been a couple of years ago.

*You have to be careful...*his, or his Mum's, words that he told me, made me inwardly furious. What made me mad was what I detected behind the subtle change in how my long-term de facto partner treated me. The implication; that I was not "one of us" but "them," those whose reactions to wealthy relations or friends could not be trusted. How dare he think that? How dare anyone imply that I'd be affected by knowing that he was an heir? As if how much money someone had, or didn't have, would affect my feelings for him, or her.

This upset me, for I had willingly sacrificed and withstood much because of my relationship with Samuel. My father did not approve, and said either I could stop seeing him or get out.

I rebelled, I left the family home; I was still only seventeen, in my final matriculation year at school. To save my relationship with my new boyfriend I'd had to run away from home and in effect give myself to him in a de facto marriage, and I just hadn't cared about what my father said, I loved him.

I was mad but I didn't say anything. Much later, I thought maybe I should have. It might have made money-matters easier to negotiate between us. Instead, I became silently resentful, and Samuel's non-spending became convoluted and perverse. As if scared people wouldn't like him for pure motives, as he was rich, he tried to never spend at all, so friends and people we met might think of us as poor, as most people we knew were. So that, in his thinking, other people would like him for being himself, despite his supposed poverty. But ironically he hardly had cheap tastes.

"Only the best for the best," Samuel said one evening in my— and his—fourth week in the house in Glenelg. It was one of his favourite phrases. He ran his hand down the length of my back. We were lying on the Persian rug he'd found in a warehouse in town, and transported with the aid of a truck he had for use with a part-time job he'd got, helping a doctor renovate. When I was at university, he'd brought the rug back to brighten-up the room, he'd said to me with a big smile. But its illegitimate presence irritated me. It annoyed me to have had, and to still be in, a serious relationship with a 'principled' kleptomaniac. Why, Samuel, don't you spend some money?

I jumped up.

"You've got to take it away," I said. "I can't have it in my room. It'll get us into trouble.

Now, I have journalism work to do, Samuel!"

I sat down at my desk and continued to write.

I wrote a review of Ray's work for the *Glenelg Gazette:*

GRIDS OF COMPLEXITY REVEAL NEW EDGE IN ART EXHIBITION

Raymond Furnett's work is showing at Laura Canyon, the cutting-edge commercial gallery in town. Furnett paints mathematical grids in primary colours. His works display the clear influence of the Australian avant-garde colour painters of the late 60s and early 70s whose leading lights included artists such as Robert Rooney and Alun Leach-Jones. Also known as Hard Edge painters, their paintings are non-representative, concrete more than abstract. They aimed to make paintings that were literally nothing more than essence of painting itself; that brought in no references from outside. The picture plane as coloured pigment on material form. In his careful painterly approach to being and nothingness, as he seeks to capture and enact the essence of painting itself, Furnett uses only primaries, red, blue, yellow, applied with an airbrush to mathematical grids of complexity revealing optical illusions that only become apparent on closer scrutiny: thus mirroring the processes of perception. Furnett's "colour studies" are, intriguingly, juxtaposed with his second genre: self-mutilating performance art.

In the overall body of Ray's work, two of the most theoretically and creatively opposed 1970s avant-garde movements came together: colour field and self-mutilation, a combination that I found intriguing and emotionally magnetic. There was nobody else I knew of who was doing conceptual visual art that was so radical and self-contradictory. His art works epitomized the word-plaudit of the time: bizarre. I interpreted his work as being a comment on reason, and a legitimate subversion, that was exciting at that time. Most exciting and gravitational of all was the enigma I saw in his work, the sense of ambiguity and mystery, which left it open to multiple different readings, like a *tabula rasa*—for my desire for new creative experience and, paradoxically, sensation.

I went to the opening of Ray's show, Double Vision, with Samuel.

Ray wasn't drinking. He looked very sober, low profile and clean cut; dressed in black, standing close to Lily wearing eau-de-nil platforms and a forest-green, swirly, almost see-through dress. He seemed preoccupied, talking quietly and intently; they left together before the gallery closed.

A few days later, I went back to the gallery on my own. Restlessly I peered and prowled past his works on the walls. As I walked, I caught flashes of my own reflection in the windows and in the glass on his prints. A ghost-pale face framed by long loose auburn hair; a tall lean angular body; old army-surplus trousers, purple velvet long-sleeved tee-shirt and ankle high Australian riding boots. I looked deeply into Raymond's work, the grids and bars, illusory geometric forms, which to my eyes did not entrap, did not stop there; instead, seeming to bend before my gaze, twisting, changing, giving way to endlessly recurring optical patterns, pathways, possibilities; letting me in to an altered state of reality, a new colour Field of vision. The feeling of excitement it gave me was like the illusion of finding a new colour that only he and I could see.

I was dancing in the living room in the dark on my own. I was the only one in, or if anyone else was, they were in bed. Sam was at vegetarian cookery class. I sang along to the urgent lyrics, *never gonna go home... never gonna go home, again, running away, with you... into the sky blue, not gonna...* I wailed with the scratchy punk voice.

I sang along, perfectly in tune with the emotion. The end of my parents' marriage, which tore our family apart after we moved to Australia, was an emotional site of memories I did not wish to return to. Dad's shouted ultimatum, after I'd been seeing Samuel for a month or so: "You can stop seeing him or get out." Leaving that night, through the window of the small bedroom I'd shared with Lily (who wasn't there because she was still in Papua New Guinea with the friends that she'd met at the alternative school where I'd met Samuel). Sam was waiting for me, dark knight on the highway, at the top of the embankment near the house. I'd secretly rung him following Dad's words. A cardboard box of clothes and school-work was tucked under my arm. I climbed onto his bike and left home. That night, I moved into my boyfriend's room in his share-house, the first of several rooms in several houses we'd lived in together over the past four years.

I couldn't stop thinking about Raymond.

Even though he was still with Lily, I couldn't help myself glancing at him when they were there. Anything of his that he left in the house, I found myself picking up, appraisingly. His comics, *Far Out Productions*; books, Cocteau's *The White Book*. Things that belonged to Ray, everything he liked, his taste, gave me that electrifying buzz I'd felt when my eyes first met his...

Margarita had begun studying photography in Melbourne at the same time that I moved to Adelaide to study arts. The last time I'd seen her, in Sydney, we'd both been visiting my sister Lily in her room in Glebe. Margy and I had walked to Glebe Point Road together. I was on my way to meet Samuel who was getting the bike fixed up at a garage before we left.

"Well, good-bye Roxy-baby," my best friend said.

She was dressed in a green-and-cream striped vintage '50s linen sundress, black hat and orange platform thongs. Her belongings were packed in her Gladstone bag and backpack. She was catching the bus to Central station.

After Samuel came and picked me up, we passed Margy, walking through the Saturday crowds on Glebe Point Road. Samuel beeped the motorbike horn, and we waved. We were riding back to Canberra then riding on to Adelaide.

...Raymond Furnett has finished art school now. But he didn't get his degree. They said his final project "wasn't Art":

Ray With Knife Stuck Through Hand—a photographic series. Yes, he really did stick a knife through his hand—a bloody great chef's knife, freshly sharpened, which he went out and chose for the purpose. His friend, Dog, snapped a few rolls of film of him in the act. Haven't seen the photos yet but I have seen Ray's hand—absolutely vile, Darling—purple, black, yellow, swollen to twice normal size, from the internal bruising. Apparently he was lucky to have missed the bones.

And it did not go down too well with the authorities. We can't award your degree, Furnett, in case it sets a precedent—what would happen if all the students stuck knives into and out-through their own body parts, eh? Mutilating themselves in the name of Art?

Imagine the carnage, Darling! Apparently they really thought it might be the start of an undergraduate blood bath.

Every time I see him at parties he's totally out of it, and I've never seen anyone make performances of excessive drinking like Ray. He's got quite a reputation, something of a cult figure, in the Art Scandals. For a short while everyone invited him and it was the sign of a cool party if he was there. But as he takes it so far, some people are turning against him now, can't handle the excess and extremes.

It's like it's his mission, his Art, to push everything beyond the limits, especially himself. You have to go beyond the boundaries to find out what the boundaries are, and so on… Yeah right. If I chop off my head, guess what! I'm dead! I'm not into self-mutilation. Anyway it's all been done before: by Spike Marr. But his other work, which he shows at Laura Canyon, is different—geometric, mathematical, optical illusions in muted, soft, primary colours, which he applies with an airbrush.

Shame you're finding the photography course too commercial. Who knows, it could be useful to be able to shoot a bar of soap from 15 different angles, some day.

How's the electric violin? Say hi to Tiimon and the band from me. We'll have to do some more busking.

See you next week when you come to stay. Maybe we'll catch up with the Lone Deranger himself—

Margarita wrote back to tell me that she hadn't met anyone very interesting in Melbourne or more to the point, that she hadn't seen anyone she remotely fancied.

She came to stay, with my sister Lily, also known as Lilt. After disappearing for months, Lily had returned from the highlands of Papua New Guinea. They had met their counterparts in the house and they met Ray; I didn't tell Lilt or Margy what I felt about Ray, my secret love desire. They knew I wanted to leave Samuel, as I'd told them, but I always found it easier to tell my close friends about my negative feelings for others, not how much I felt for other people. To me, that felt like a betrayal of my feelings for all concerned.

Ray seemed to be hanging out everywhere. No longer with Lily, no longer living at Rubicon Road, he was on a critically subversive cultural rampage. Immaculately painted murals of activist heroes, or anti-corporate slogans would appear mysteriously overnight on walls around the city. If I heard The Art Scandals were supposed to be creating a performance, for instance heckling at The Arts Playhouse, "Bourgeois rubbish!" "Boring!" "Go home!" "Get a job!" "Boo! Boo!" until they were told to leave; or rumour had it they were playing a gig; I would suggest to Samuel that we go along—to see if there was anything happening. If I was invited to go to an opening or an art party—and there were happenings all the time—I insisted to Samuel that I had to go. We went together on the bike. He wore his black leather jacket, with jeans or black leather trousers. I sat behind him, like I always did, pressed against Samuel's back, hands on his thighs, or tucked into the front pockets in his trousers.

At the endless art happenings, after Lily Rosser had left Ray, I witnessed the second genre of his art practice: self-mutilation.

He had a fetish for "broken glass."

At that time, I wanted to interpret this as a cool statement on the impossibility of pure and transparent construction in an imperfect world. In other words, the inverse, or mirror opposite, of his colour field works, in which he sought to find the essence of painting. The way I had wanted to interpret his performance was that his attitude to Art making was symbolized in two significant actions. Firstly, he drank to excess from bottles of alcohol; then, he broke the emptied bottles in a performance that was impromptu, and had the shock of immediacy. At a squat happening where some of the Art Scandals were staying, a party, I watched his performance, from a slight distance. It was very late. The light bulbs had no shades. The floorboards had no covering. A few people were present. Raymond was smashing bottles, shouting enigmatic artistic conundrums:

"Watch the negative shapes...Watch the negative space..."

Before the arrival of local police—who regarded the place with astonishment before leaving without doing anything— Raymond turned to me, and said words that, oddly, affirmed me. And which astonished me.

"She's magnificent. Look at her! She's not afraid to look."

And I knew that this was it.

What I felt was not love.

It could not be "Love." Ever since the parents had separated I'd found, to my surprise, that I couldn't say the word "Love" without feeling deeply uneasy and self-conscious, like a kind of shame: of the family splitting up.

To protect my own relationships, it was as if I had to view them as existing in a different realm to the world of "Love" in which families had existed, and shattered in. My family was very idealistic. My mother had been devoted to my father, and I was brought up on regular doses of 'happy family' ideology, administered like preventative health care. Ingrained into me from an early age, was the myth of the never-ending love of my parents for each other, and the solidity of the family unit. The myth was exploded conclusively when Dad left Mum for his young research assistant shortly after we moved from the Old World to Canberra.

When Rimbaud was 19 and the older poet Verlaine was 27 they fell violently in love. Verlaine left his wife and ran off with Rimbaud. From Paris they travelled to London where they lived in a terrace house next to a narrow alleyway in Camden Town. For two weeks they lived and loved and fought and drank and screwed. And then Verlaine shot Rimbaud in the hand, and they moved on. Apart.

I had been kicked out. Mum was left with my two younger sisters and younger brother in a small bungalow on the farthest outskirts, newest suburb, in the Australian Capital Territory. It was stark. The bungalow had been allocated to Dad by the government when he took up his post in the nation's capital.

It was supposed to be temporary accommodation, until Dad and Mum bought a suitable, bigger, family house. They did buy a shack in the mountains. But there never would be a new house for our family.

And I was on my own.

"Raymond dancing his ballet on broken glass," said Tel, one of the Art Scandals, one night as a group of us watched Ray stagger and twirl like a dervish in a trance. Like a punk Nijinsky, I thought as I sipped spring water, marvelling at his obvious and deeply artistic pain.

When I watched him at those parties I wanted to think I had the sensation of looking into a human mirror. What I saw in the image of Ray was my desire for unknown pleasures, in an exaggerated form. Repeated in a desire that was catching. Just being in the vicinity of Ray, or knowing that people were expecting him, and that I might see him, set my nerve endings jangling with anticipation.

And as for his talk about Evil, what did he mean by that? I was the recipient of a liberal-arts education, I did not believe in binary oppositions, although it is true that I did, most certainly, want to believe in Good. I assumed that Ray's use of the word was intentionally provocative, an ironic part of his artistic performance.

Around the end of first semester
As I was writing at my desk, with the door to my room ajar, Fraser said my name. I turned around and heard a click as he photographed me.

"Smile!" he said smiling. He clicked a few times.

I smiled in politely hidden mild irritation, and returned to my writing.

He did not ever show me the photographs, and I forgot all about it. That was around the end of first semester, or was it the start of second semester, after Lily left.

I didn't think much of it at the time. People who were photographers who I knew were always looking for the money shot, or art shot. They had to take snaps when they thought they had an image perfectly framed in their camera viewfinder. No doubt Fraser was too. Of course, it did not occur to me to suspect he might have had a more sinister agenda.

One night Fraser and I were sitting in front of the wood fire in the living room, drinking his champagne. He had several bottles and had offered me a glass, and I had accepted. It was the first time we had talked at length, and a little depth. We were chatting, gazing into the fiery scapes of embers and flame, and somehow the conversation turned to accidents.

I told him about an accident I had been in. To me, nothing could be more terrible and riveting than this. He listened with avid attention. He told me about a motorbike accident he was in the year before that affected his nervous system, which has left him with a slight hand tremor.

"It was last year. I was studying Architecture. In Melbourne. After the accident I couldn't draw anymore. So that's why I am studying Art."

"Oh…" I empathized.

We drank bottles of champagne and next day I felt as if I had been burnt from within, huddled in bed willing time to pass and take me beyond this, hangover did not describe it.

Not long after that. I was in the kitchen making coffee. Margarita waltzed in with a bag of shopping. She put items on her food shelves neatly.

"Umeboshi plums." She placed the jar on the shelf in front of me. Followed by six jars precisely.

"Aren't they s'posed to be good for hangovers?" Wished I'd had some after that night drinking champers.

"I don't know. I don't drink," she said, rather primly.

"Are you baking?"

Margarita used the oven, she'd made scones and apple cake that only she and Fraser ate.

"I've got a craving," she said in a clipped tone.

She was always quite particular and neat, and that defined her style. That day she was wearing a tangerine sweater over a cream blouse with a tiny floral pattern, the collar of which was tucked over the cashmere neckline, sleeves pulled up revealing the cuffs of her blouse; and a three-quarter length dark skirt, over brown leather boots. I liked her appearance, it reminded me of English girls in the '70s, a pulled-together style, she'd said her father was from India, he'd met her mother in Bristol, the city near where my family had lived when I was a child. She had black hair, piercing brown eyes, and pale skin. Yes, she looked a little similar to "my" Margarita.

Margarita had told me the story of leaving her husband; she'd told all of us one evening when we were playing Art Scrabble. All the words had to be connected to art, it was Lily's idea and typical of her.

"Leonardo!!" called Lily, placing her letters. "Double word score! 63 points!"

"That's my husband's name," Margarita said. We all looked at her.

"Is he Italian?" asked Lily.

"No, English. We met when he was on holiday, and staying in Castlemaine, at the hotel, where I grew up. I was seventeen. He was nineteen on an overseas student exchange."

Margarita continued, to surprised attention: "I was married at eighteen. My husband stayed in Australia after we met. We visited his family on our honeymoon. They lived in a stately home in Dorset that was in their family for hundreds of years; they sold it to Lon Jennono the singer."

"Really?" said Lily.

Fraser coughed.

"He's paying me an allowance," she added. "But I won't go back. I was too young. I want freedom to do my own thing, like go to art school."

"Let's get on with this game," said Fraser.

"I was seventeen and Sam was nineteen when we first met."

"B-R-U-S-H. 4 points!" said Sam.

Fraser groaned.

"Can't you do anything smarter?" said Lily, "SMARTER!! Art-er, err? Geddit?"

* * *

"I have to eat them." She picked up a spoon and scooped out a dollop of pickled plum, which she popped into her mouth.

"Do you eat them on their own like that?"

"They're pickles. I like them like this," she called back over her shoulder as she sauntered out of the kitchen, carrying the jar and spoon.

After Margarita had left the kitchen, I reached up, and took down one of the jars of plums. I had eaten these in Japan. But that was a few years ago. I turned the jar around and squinted at the fine print.

> Umeboshi plums are a salty pickled plum that originated in China three thousand years ago. Legend has it that a dried salted plum or uboi was found in a tomb built 2900 years ago. These piquant pickles are famous for their health giving properties; they act as an alkalizer, that clears toxins, eliminates fatigue, and slows the ageing process.

So these were, in a way, food of the dead. Found in tombs, and believed to prolong life.

Maybe I should start to eat them too. I daren't try one now

though, she would be bound to notice.

By the end of the week I noticed only two jars were left.

The following week—like every one of Margarita's belongings—all the jars of pickled plums were gone.

* * *

I didn't talk often with Margarita. She was always busy rushing in, rushing out, as was I; though I spent more time in the house, in my room writing.

Another time I remember I had been making coffee. I was using a mug that Sam had brought back from his work at the doctor's, he said they were clearing out an old kitchen, and it was being thrown out.

A crab image was printed on one side. *Introverted, sensitive, yet brave loyal friends, Cancerians are the quiet achievers of the zodiac.* The gold words circled the dark blue mug.

"Gee, I like your cup," said Margarita looking at it closely.

"It was being thrown out," I said, "Sam got it from where he's working."

"Gee." She said again, annoyingly.

"What's your rising sign?" she asked. "The planet that was in the ascendant, rising into view in the sky, at the moment that you were born."

"I have no idea," I said.

Although I read my horoscope in magazines and newspapers, that was for fun. Same as when I asked people I had just met what star sign they were, it was a kind of a joke more than anything else. It gave a starting point for conversation.

"Hold on a minute, I'm going to get something that might interest you."

She hurried out and returned with a paperback book with a

yellow pattern of constellations in the night sky and a leaping goat on the cover that even I knew represented a "star sign."

"Now. When and where were you born?" she asked

Inwardly, I sighed. I was supposed to be finishing an essay. I had just been reading that Jung believed in astrology and the I-Ching. I might as well continue the conversation.

"1960. Eighth of July, in London."

"Gee. You're four years younger than me."

I felt oddly irritated. Would she stop saying that word?

She opened the book, ran her finger down a page staring in concentration. She tapped the page then announced.

"Gee-whiz, Roxy. Your rising sign is Leo. Sun sign Cancer. Cancer-Leo, Moon and Sun. Two opposites."

She read from the book:

" 'On the outside you may appear to be quiet, demure, shy, introverted and timid, but inside you have a fire burning that will light up the sky if you let it. This can confuse people when you start to blaze your trail, and you are often misunderstood, thought to be a troublemaker and rebel, when in fact you are an artist.' "

I had been prepared to brush it off and laugh politely, but there was something accurate in that.

"I'm Taurus, with Pisces rising, I'm a bull in a china shop on the outside, also sturdy and strong and practical, but inside sensitive, creative, dreamy. The outside protects the inner me."

For a moment I thought she had said 'creamy' like a marshmallow inside.

"Oh, right," I said politely, not quite sure how to respond to this self-perception of my umeboshi-addicted housemate as a raging bull with a dreamy creamy inside.

"Astrology is just a symbolic language, it's a way of communicating to people about the self, on a deeper level without being deep, if you get me."

"Yes, that makes more sense. I've been reading about it for an essay. Jung believed in astrology, as a way of approaching or understanding dreams and the inner world of the collective unconscious."

"Hmm. I am doing a series of slow shutter speed portraits from my major work. Would you model for me? We could do a performance art project where you are the artist and I take the photographs?"

"Yes, okay... I've done performance projects with my sister and our friends. Margarita, my friend, I told you about, who has the same name and star sign as you, takes the photos. She's started studying photography now, this year, in Melbourne."

We did the photo shoot or the performance art project, whichever way you looked at it, the following week, at the art school, in a studio space in front of a mirror. Margarita and I went there together on the tram.

Sitting at the back, where there were no other people, she said suddenly, "When you were talking to Fraser last week, at night, in front of the fire, did he tell you about what happened to him?"

"His accident?"

"Yes." Her eyes were boring into me like the beady eyes of a robin. The birds I used to watch hopping around, and fed, in the garden in England, in the snow in winter.

"Yes, he did." We were getting off the tram now.

"Did he tell you *why* he was speeding on his motorbike, and why he didn't see the bus that ran into him?" she said, as we were walking towards the art school. Her voice was tense, but she always sounded a bit uptight.

"No." I said.

"Is this it?" I gestured unnecessarily towards the Victorian Gothic building.

"Yes," she said impatiently. "Fraser was being abused. You know his father died when he was four. A friend of his family began abusing him when he was ten. He lived in Melbourne, he was—is—an economist. He worked at the University of Commerce in Melbourne. He was Jewish, had been in a concentration camp in the War. According to Fraser, he was in what was called the Special Squad. The Jewish prisoners who carried out the killings of fellow inmates inside the concentration camps, they did it for scraps of food, and alcohol, to survive. Some of the victims became like the perpetrators. He survived and he migrated to Australia. He started to befriend or "groom" Fraser when Fraser was having problems with Maths; Frase ran away from home when he was fourteen and lived with the man in his house in Melbourne. I think he is part of the rings of abuse, the Brotherhood, in Melbourne and Adelaide now. The terrible things, abductions, disappearances, murders of teenage boys, no-one is talking about. There were several other teenagers who were at the man's house. He was teaching them business skills, he said, so they could support themselves. It had been going on for years. Fraser was running away from him when he had his accident. As he was riding his motorbike, he was crying so much he could not see the bus."

"God," I exclaimed.

"Don't let Fraser know I told you," she said. "But I think it's important that people know what is going on here. The things that no one is talking about, because they're too scared."

Her voice was intense, urgent.

"That's terrible," I said.

I was shocked by her words, and that she should be saying this about Fraser. I didn't know what to say.

We went into the building. I dressed up in some peasant-looking clothes in her studio. Margarita took photographs. I felt a little uneasy that she had told me what she had about Fraser. Why did she want to say that? I wanted to think it wasn't true. Though why would she want to make up something like that? And, whether it was true or not, and I had a horrible feeling it was true, why tell me? Even though she wasn't scared, obviously she felt worried. But what could I do about it? Nothing. It had nothing to do with me. It was all very unsettling.

Margarita showed me one of the images about three weeks later, one morning in the living room as I was on my way out to university. It wasn't at all like I expected. She had taken the shot as I was turning my head; her image portrayed my face as completely missing, all I could see was a blurred outline of my hair and the rough shape of my head, in images that had been superimposed, so that my face disappeared.

"This is the one I'm using for my end of semester project," she said.

"That's great," I replied politely, not entirely meaning it. It was disturbing. Because it was me. Or, rather, it wasn't. "Interesting effect."

That was the only one of the images she showed me from the series of photos she took.

Not long after that, Margarita disappeared. She left without saying a word about leaving. I came back from university one evening and she was gone.

There were no jars of plums on the shelf. Her kitchen shelf was empty.

Fraser was almost rude when I asked him about Margarita. He muttered, he didn't know; he sounded on edge. What was going on?

She'd stayed in Fraser's room, and no one took her place.

Lily disappeared a month later, or was it the month before. It was after she said she was ending her affair with Raymond. A few days later when I returned to the house after a day at the university, the door to her room was open and the room was cleared of all her things, her kitchen shelf was empty, and she was gone.

Fraser said she left because she was not seeing Raymond anymore; he said she'd said she was leaving the art school and starting again, taking secretarial studies in another city next year. That's all she'd told him.

"When did she say that?" I was surprised. It was the first I had heard about it, she'd not mentioned anything to me and we had chatted often.

"The electricity bill needs to be paid," he said changing the subject abruptly and aggressively.

"I gave you my contribution to the bill last week, Fraser," I said. "Have you forgotten?"

"Roxy gave you her share of the bill last week, remember?" Samuel said walking into the living room.

"Oh, yeah, she did. Things on my mind."

"Well get them off your mind," Samuel said, "Don't accuse Roxy."

Fraser stomped out of the room almost tripping on a piece

of coconut matting. Next day Fraser showed the room to a young surfer, Kyle, who moved in the day after with a bong collection, and surfboard.

First Margarita had disappeared without a word. No. It was Lily first, then Margarita.

"People move on," said Samuel. "Their relationships ended and they left. It's not exactly a mystery."

"Margarita's relationship with Fraser didn't end." I said.

"Yes it did. He told me. She left him."

"Oh. That's different then." But still I found it unsettling.

* * *

I concerned myself with studying. There was a strong Marxist influence in the Philosophy department in the university. I wrote on Taoism, and on Dialectics from Hegel's Transcendental Idealism to Marx's Materialism. Our lecturer held tutorials in the university bar, and we discussed Marxist theory applied to social problems, unfortunately he was not well, and was absent often on sick leave, as he had picked up malaria in his travels to Asia, he told us. He held a party at his house, which I attended, and walked around joining in several discussions on the philosophy of the Aboriginal Rights movement; and the efficacy of direct-action sit-ins as a form of protest for social change, and the anti-Vietnam War moratorium protests a few years before (which Samuel had been to).

In English, I wrote a review of Sylvia Plath's poetry, and an essay on James Joyce's *Portrait of the Artist as a Young Man* and *Dubliners,* but found it frustrating to be far away, and not able to hear the sound and rhythms of voices of Dubliners, to gain the full meaning and resonance of the text.

In Drama, the syllabus had a strong European influence.

One day, I arrived a little late and missed the usual introductions. I did not know the film we were going to be watching. I slipped into the theatre. I anticipated it might be a European avant-garde bucolic romance, as I could see on the screen the handheld camera tracking through a beautiful forest, then suddenly with no preparation, the viewer, I, was plunged into the horror incarnate of the Nazi atrocities. It was the highly significant film *Nuit et brouillard* (Night and Fog) by Alain Resnais, with sound track by Hanns Eisler. The film included footage from newsreels of the time. Footage from Auschwitz concentration camp showed images filmed by Nazi SS guards. Massive piles of emaciated corpses, and the SS guards smiling and laughing. I could hardly force myself to watch. When it had ended, I stumbled out, shaken to have learnt about the horrific images. A history of the Second World War, and background to the lives of many refugees in Australia, including Samuel's family, that I had known little about, at least not in such graphic detail.

In the class afterwards, our lecturer talked to us about the film's German-translation narration by the poet Paul Celan who was a Romanian-Jewish survivor of imprisonment in a slave-labour camp in the holocaust writing his poem *Todesfuge* (Death-fugue) based on Nazi death camps where musicians were forced by the "meister" to play as prisoners dug graves— forced by the commander that he configured as "a master from Deutschland". The most intense art was made in Europe, and I was studying it, in Adelaide.

I read more widely and discovered disturbing things. In the Second World War in the Nazi regime, in the newly formed state of Croatia, under the Ustasha fascists, hundreds of thousands of Jews, Gypsies, and Serbs were killed in concentration camps. The killings were barbaric, in villages and towns. There were travelling fairs and carnivals; special trucks were made to look like sideshows of magicians' displays or halls of mirrors. The vans were disguised extermination units. Gas jets were turned on and those inside were murdered, and disappeared. My heart lurched and I felt faint as I read this. Was this why fairgrounds had sometimes been depicted as sites of horror, in films, I had picked up on it subliminally but like most people had no inkling of this horrific history. I'd thought it was just the terrifying contrast, of fun and murder. After reading that, the local funfair appeared disturbing to me. I didn't know that I might be psychic.

Then by extraordinary serendipity, or as if it was meant to happen, I was suddenly told a lot more about this gruesome chapter in history which brought it right into the present, and place where I was living.

I went to another artists' party with Samuel on his bike. When we walked in, I was surprised at how quiet it was. Several people were in the main room, lit by candles, soft Greek music was playing. There was food in the kitchen, ratatouille, and bowls of dips, and bottles of wine, and beer. We helped ourselves to ratatouille, and I walked back into the main room. Diana, a friend of Ray's and his friends, who'd moved to Sydney, was talking and the people around her were listening avidly. I sat on the couch in front of her. I liked Diana; she was tall and slim, with black feathered hair gelled into spiny anteater spikes; she was wearing army surplus store overalls. Her art was forceful; she was one of the mural painters whose works were so daring, bold and relevant. She was in a relationship with one of Ray's colleagues. She was staying in town for a few days, before she returned to Sydney. She was laughing, telling everyone about an exchange of views she'd had in a forum with a critic none of the artists liked. Then her tone grew more serious, low and urgent.

"Some off things have been happening. A guy moved in to the house next to Art Squat. We've got permission to stay there right, and use the place until it's turned into apartments, right? This guy is in his sixties, I'd say. He's disabled. Has a motorised chair. Introduced himself, on the street, said he's called Branko. He asked what we're doing, you know I like to be friendly with neighbours. I said we're artists, right? We'd be using the space as a studio for the foreseeable. A few days later he pushed his way into the studio. Left his chair in the front yard. Hopped off, swaggered in with a mild limp. Talk about assertive. Aggressive. Says he was in the Ustasha in Croatia, a fascist regime founded by the Nazis and Italians. Then, off the cuff, he launches into a litany of the things, unbelievable gross things he says he did in the Second World War. The things he said he did. I can't repeat. Makes me sick to think about it. We don't know why he'd tell us these things. It's like he's trying to intimidate us, scare us. It's creepy."

"What kind of things?" said a guy with cropped hair in a red leather jacket and red jeans.

"Couldn't you say anything to give just an idea?" asked a girl with short spiky red hair.

"Well you'd better not blame me if it makes you spew up your ratatouille," said Diana.

"We won't, it's good for us to know what's going on, if he's trying to intimidate young artist, that's serious," said the same guy.

"We're not sure what he's trying to do," Diana said. "And it's probably good, the more people know about it the better. In case anything happens. Okay. He said—" She paused.

"He said he was in a raid on a school in a village, which had been in Yugoslavia or Slovenia. The Ustasha fascists gave orders to kill Serbs, communists. He said they did barbaric things, to the children with knives. Gouging out eyes. Right there in the classroom. It was part of the genocide."

"Ugh! Don't go on," said the girl with short red hair.

"Yes, that's enough horror," said the guy in red.

I was almost regurgitating the ratatouille.

"He said he did that. He told us as if he was proud, and he was jeering at us, right?"

Then as we were sitting there, and I was almost disbelieving it, the artist in red leather trousers said:

"I've heard that war criminals were allowed into Australia after the Second World War, if they were anti-communist. Many hundreds of Nazis, and fascists left Europe via rat runs that's what their hidden escape routes were called. Sanctioned by the Catholic Church, they were protected, sheltered in safe houses, in monasteries, and in the Vatican, given 'Persil passports', bleached international passports by the Red Cross, and they escaped trial in Europe for their crimes. They assumed false identities in countries such as South America. Canada. Australia. Your neighbour might have been connected to that. I believe some fascists and Nazi war criminals were recruited to work in the Snowy Mountains Scheme, after the war."

"Jeepers," said Diana. "Right. He did say he was a fascist."

"The worse thing is that some of them were recruited to the government spy agencies. They target groups including artists and writers. They had it in for modernists in the 1940s."

"How do you know this?" I could not stop myself from asking. Modernists?

"His father had connections," said Diana.

"My family has a farm, an old shack, in the foothills of the Snowy Mountains!" They ignored my comment,

"Do you think he might be spying on us? Even though we're postmodernists?" Diana raised her left eyebrow humorously.

"It's possible," he said. "But why they'd bother I don't know. Except of course to make money. It's a job. An economy. They get paid to spy on 'persons of interest', write up stories about them. They make things up to 'gild the lily,'" he made mocking scare quotes with his fingers, "they do it to make it look like they're doing important work, to keep themselves in work."

"That's disgusting." I said vehemently. (Though I wondered how he could know all this).

"So you think he could be making up things about our Art Squat studio and reporting us to who or what exactly?"

"There's a department that deals with all of this, they keep records, and keep people under surveillance. It's to do with the Cold War," said the guy in red.

"There's worse things going on, I have heard that some of these people are involved in the abduction and murders of young people, that are happening here in Adelaide," he added.

"WHAT people?" Diana said.

"Some of the people from Europe who were allowed out, the war criminals. Some of them have wormed into very high positions. Some of them have very sick tastes, a blood lust."

He paused. Then he said, suddenly: "Something happened to me when I was hitching. I only just escaped.

"It was a few years ago, not long after my father died.

My mother couldn't cope. I'd just come out of staying in an orphanage. I'd been to an anti-Vietnam war protest, and then I went out to a poetry meeting, and was going home. I was hitchhiking alone. The man who picked me up (who could have been in his sixties), stopped the car in a deserted place in a car park by the river. He assaulted me. Sexually. I kicked him, managed to open the door and ran for my life. A few days later I saw the news about a teenager who had been murdered, his body dumped in the river, washed up on the bank. That could have been me. I was very, very lucky to get away. The murders in the news are of a similar type, and no one has been caught."

"How do you know he had anything to do with the spies?" said Diana.

"That man had a strong central European accent," the guy in red replied.

"No one knows what's happening," said the young woman.

"The teenage boy whose body was found was mutilated, in the way that you said the man who's moved in next door to you said he mutilated the school children, Diana. Sounds like the bodies that have been found recently too."

"Right," she said. "That's horrific."

"Be careful," he said. "You're too old for them. But even so be careful."

"It sounds like a spy thriller or a murder slash horror film," I said, still finding it hard to believe them.

"It's real," he said, "Haven't you been following the news?"

"No, actually I haven't."

"Well start to, and you'll see."

"My father was in the war in Germany, but he was Jewish," said Samuel suddenly to my surprise.

"He was on his way to school in England when the war

broke out. He was in a ship and it was torpedoed off the coast of Dover. Dad had to swim to shore. Later, my grandparents came to Australia, and he joined them. He was studying to be a lawyer. But he was caught after curfew returning library books, and was not allowed to study law after that."

It was a story he'd told me several times, and its familiarity was reassuring, in this very disturbing conversation.

At that moment Raymond burst into the room, laughing. "What's going on in here, an encounter group?"

"Just encountering the horror of everyday life in suburban Australia," said Diana.

What kind of everyday was this, here? Not one I wanted to have anything to do with.

I suddenly felt sick. As if I was on a roller coaster that was hurtling downwards, my stomach flipping over.

But the sight of Ray made me feel better. I associated him with the freedom of new ways of seeing and being, the progressive possibilities of art as an enlightening life force, a way to make meaning and sense from the chaos, though why I made these associations I didn't know, that was part of the attraction, the mystery which drew me to him.

"Roxy we'd better go, it's after eleven," Samuel said.

"Are you sure?"

"Yes, I've got to work tomorrow morning. And take you to your class before that."

The enlightening power of Ray, on me, had been sufficient to counter the horrors I had just heard that had almost made me throw up but ten minutes before.

When Samuel and I returned to Rubicon Road, we made hot chocolate and drank it, with the creaking of the big wheel on the other side of the road audible through the wall.

"That was horrific, what that guy said, and Diana."

"Yes," he said. "There're some sick people around."

"I hope it doesn't give me nightmares."

He gave me a hug. "You've got me to keep them away."

In July, Lily sent a letter saying she'd decided to move to Amsterdam to join an avant-garde theatre company we'd heard about when we'd given a lift to a guy hitchhiking when we were driving to the Farm, the year before. The guy was European and he'd told us about an English-speaking theatre company on a canal that Lily had not forgotten. She'd made it her mission to go there and join. She had saved for her one-way ticket by busking on inner Sydney streets. She'd met a violinist who played music hall. She'd approached him, said she liked his music, and asked if she could accompany him, they rehearsed a routine and sang and played music hall songs, on the streets around Central Station; she made the fare to leave the country after six months. Through only eating fruit and vegetables thrown out by the local greengrocer on Glebe Point Road. And the chokoes that grew on the rooftop outside her window, she ate them boiled or steamed.

Lily visited in August, in farewell. Margy and Edwin, one of the Papua New Guinea tribe, all came to my place, to stay, to say goodbye to Lily.

She wrote letters, from Amsterdam, to say that she'd gone to the theatre company, and she'd been accepted to work with them, but was suffering personal trouble adjusting to reality and was going to Northern Ireland to stay with Bee, her best friend from when we lived there, to get her feet back on the ground. Then, a few weeks later, she wrote to say she'd heard of a method-acting theatre company in Dublin, run by Maeve

McCreedy, an actress-cum-director from a European studio in New York, who'd trained with Melville Brandi.

* * *

It was around then that I had a surprise visit from two police officers that came to the house to search my room. Fraser had lied about me to the police. He lied that I had drugs in my room. They searched and, off course, found nothing as I never took drugs and hated drugs. Samuel was out when they came around. I stood as they looked in the fireplace, up the chimney, in my papers, under the mattress on the floor. Then they left. So many things were going on, and it was so far removed from my life, that I did not even think about it afterwards.

Not long after that I had another surprise visitor. It was one afternoon in second semester. I caught a bus to the university. It stopped at the edge of the campus, which was set in rolling landscaped grounds. A path led to the college buildings. As I was walking towards a grassy knoll, I saw sitting on the grass, not a gnome on a toadstool, but a familiar figure staring at me with dark hooded eyes. Carl. Gazing at me as if transfixed.

Carl was why I had left Samuel two years ago in Adelaide when we were travelling around Australia and had just ridden down through the desert. I hadn't been able to stop thinking about him as we rode up the east coast and over the Atherton Tablelands, through the remote mining towns, Mount Isa and Mackay, the outback known as 'the Top', and down through the central desert; and our platonic romantic affair, if it could be called that. I had gone back to Canberra by train to Carl. It hadn't worked out. I found that he'd moved in with my sister; they were sharing a house with a guitarist. We tried to talk, it all fell flat, and then he moved to Sydney with his band. Now

Raymond was occupying all my romantic thoughts.

What was Carl doing here? I thought with shock.

He stood up slowly and walked towards me.

"Roxy." He said in the presumptuous, commanding, domineering tone he had, whilst acting besotted. "How are ya?"

"Hi Carl. What are you doing here?"

Out on this hill, in South Australia, we might as well have been in the middle of nowhere.

"I came to see you."

"Where are you living now?"

"Sydney. Still in the same place in Glebe."

He gazed at me. Something didn't seem right. I was more than a little uncomfortable. Why was he here? I was in a hurry and had to get to class.

"How's it going here?"

"Everything's fine. Great." I tried to make an effort. "How are you?"

He suddenly hooked his index fingers in the belt loops of my jeans and pulled me to him.

I gasped in shock.

"*Do you know how much you mean to me?*" His voice was low and insistent, but rasping.

I jumped away from him.

"I thought we'd decided that was all over."

"All over? I've just travelled one and a half thousand kilometres by train to see you."

I looked at him.

"How did you know where I'd be?"

"Uh," he looked rather uneasy. "I rang the university, and said I knew you, and asked them where you'd be."

I stared at him.

"I asked them where and when your lectures were, and I worked it out."

I was surprised they'd given out my details to someone just ringing and asking.

"Well. I have to go now. I have to get to my class."

"Your class?" he said in a tone of disbelief and anger.

"Yes, I must go. I have to go now. I'll be late."

I was backing away.

I left him on that windswept hill, staring at me inscrutably, looking none too pleased.

I was sure he didn't come all that way on the off chance of seeing me. Later I remembered that his father was high up in police agencies. I didn't think about it then, but much later I remembered his odd visit, not long after Fraser had maliciously lied to the police that I had drugs, doing all he thought he could to get me into trouble, serious trouble as it turned out. And I realized that my psychic instinct for danger was correct. It was to prove to be not just a "coincidence."

But I didn't see Carl for a while.

My feelings for Raymond Furnett, underground though they were, had not abated. I still dreamed about him with a crackle of excitement racing through my nervous system as if he was something—a fever, a mood—I was genetically or otherwise destined to catch.

2

An end-of-year party was held in the big two-floor student house at the corner of Rubicon Road. I called in to the party with Samuel. As we walked in, right before my eyes, in front of us, stood Ray and friends in the Art Scandals, drinking and laughing. I could sense Samuel's psychic aggression-defensive reflex; he kept close to me, pressed to me, wouldn't move away, even when I wanted to dance he insisted on dancing with me.

"Hi Raymond," he said. It was strange. Over the last few months he had become friendlier with Ray than I was.

I went upstairs to go to the bathroom.

When I came out of the bathroom, Raymond was in the hallway. I walked past him casually.

"G'day," he said. He looked at me from behind his pale-rimmed glasses. I noticed they were bound at the bridge with clear sticky tape, another conceptual statement on transparency, transience and perception, another late-night breaking glass episode. I walked out onto the balcony. He followed me.

"What do you think of the party?" I asked him.

The sky above sparkled; galaxies of distant possible worlds beckoned... I had what Margy, Lily and I called a wonderful feeling: that tonight, anything might happen...

"Bunch of zombies," he said. "This place breeds them like a swamp." He laughed.

I laughed.

"We're going to score, do you want to buy anything?" he said, as his friend Johnny walked across the room.

"So you're coming back here?" I said.

"Yeah, should do, in an hour or so, we're getting speed, dope..."

"No thanks," I smiled. He smiled back.

"Are you staying around?"

"Yeah, I think I will, for a while."

"See you later on." He looked at me again—meaningfully and the meaning was exciting—and then he turned and followed John-Boy.

After they'd left, I, too, went downstairs. Samuel was in the kitchen, leaning against the sink, glass of orange juice in his hand, talking to Zac the ringletted hippy about how not to pick mangoes from a tall tree.

"Roxy, d'you remember, in Cairns," Samuel said. "I decided to pick some mangoes, not with that pole with the wire hook, and climbed the old mango tree near the youth hostel, it was about fifteen metres high, and the branch I was standing on broke, and I would have fallen all the way to the ground, if I hadn't grabbed onto that other branch..."

"Yes, I do," I said vaguely, standing next to him.

"Raymond's gone," he said. "He and his mates just left."

"Really?" I poured myself a glass of organic spring water.

Then Samuel said: "I'm tired, I think I'll go back to the house."

"I think I'll stay on a bit longer. I've got too much energy to sleep. I feel like staying up for a while."

I walked around the downstairs rooms and upstairs rooms of the house, up and down the wide sweeping staircase; there was no one I knew. But I felt too restless to go back. I left the party, and headed off down to the pier, past the silent fairground. Deserted and full of shadows, it looked like the set of a horror movie.

I walked along the pier, out into the black night water of the Bay. Small waves rolled on their way to shore on either side of me. Down on the beach a few people from the party were swimming. A girl with cropped bleached hair stripped off her dress, screamed, and ran shrieking into the waves. A couple of fishermen hunched stoically, rods balanced at sharp angles against the wooden railings. After a while, of staring at the sea, yachts, and sky, I turned and strolled slowly back to shore.

When I walked back into the party, he was there.

I was upstairs, dancing. Very loud techno-music shook the air like a sound-wave tornado. I hadn't taken any of the drugs Ray and Johnny brought. Tonight I felt, as I always did, that my consciousness could take me further than any chemicals. Ray was dancing in front of me. I was so close to him.

Then, forcefully, he put his hands on my shoulders, leaned over and kissed me. I tasted its sudden shock.

He pulled back, mumbling, "Let's find a room. Come on, there's one this way..."

I followed him out of the room of dancers across the top hallway to the door that he was opening.

We entered a comfortable bedroom; softly lit by a lamp on a low table, next to a big brass bed, like the song *Lady Lay...*

"Perfect." Raymond gestured to the double bed covered with a freshly laundered blue and white striped duvet.

"Yeah, nice room," I said glancing around.

He lay down and I lay next to him. Kissing was proceeding with passion, clothing loosened, panting, his hand, my breast, his body heat, my hand, something wonderful, when suddenly the mood was broken.

"What the *hell* do you think you're doing?" a woman's irate voice demanded.

Raymond and I scrambled to get under the duvet.

"This is someone's *bedroom!*" The voice continued. "How dare you! Get *out* from under there. *That's not your bed!*"

"She said we could," Raymond said.

"What do you mean? Who said you could, what?"

"The woman who has this room. She said we could come here."

"She's not here tonight!" snapped the woman's voice. "She's away for three days! This is unbelievable. *What kind of animals are you?* To just go into other people's bedrooms and screw on their beds?"

"O God," I groaned and buried my face in the pillow.

Rimbaud stood by the window gazing onto the dingy London streetscape. His hand bandaged with Verlaine's—what? His underpants? His sock?

"Is there anywhere else we could go," asked Raymond.

"There's a room on the landing on the stairs," the woman's voice said grudgingly, after a short pause. "Now just get out."

We got up. A woman stood by the door, glaring in theatrical fury, like a demented prison warden, until we left the room.

A silence had fallen between us.

"That was 'bad luck'," I said.

"Yeah."

In the light of the hallway I noticed his face was incredibly pale.

"Where is this room she was talking about?" he added.

We hurried down a few stairs to the landing. There was a waist high door to what looked a low cupboard built into the wall. Ray pushed it open. Inside was a small, cramped, airless space. We squeezed in, he pulled the door shut. Stiflingly hot and stuffy, it was hard to breathe.

"Is there a light?"

"Can't see one!"

"What is this place?"

"Maybe it's something to do with the heating or hot water system—is that a water tank?"

"Oh yeah, right."

We started kissing again. It was pitch black and impossible to see anything.

"Let's lie down," he said. Trying not to lose balance, I sank beside him, uncomfortably onto the floor.

"It's concrete!"

"Just a minute." I felt him pulling off his tee-shirt. "This'll make it softer."

I sensed Ray was spreading his tee-shirt on the floor, and I lay beside him. It was extremely uncomfortable.

"From heaven to hell," he said, with a grim little laugh.

He moved on top of me. I was breathless and so was Ray.

Not just from passion, but because it was sweltering. The oxygen in the space was diminishing rapidly. I was panting, gasping...

"*Vite! let's make love before we cark it!*"

I said the words dramatically, in my best Eastern European punk diva voice.

Afterwards, he said, "That was beautiful anyway. Wherever we were it would have been beautiful." We kissed again, until I was practically blacking out. Opening the cupboard door, I fell out, followed by Ray, coughing, gulping down mouthfuls of fresh air.

We stood in the hallway, gasping, adjusting our clothing.

"I don't know how I'm going to get home," he said.

"Stay at our house. There's a sofa-thing. Margarita always sleeps there when she comes to stay."

"What about Samuel?"

"Exactly. Samuel will be asleep. Samuel went back ages ago because he was tired. What's the time now?"

"I don't have a watch."

We walked out from the house, and onto the street. Rising above the rooftops we could see the clock tower on the Town Hall.

"Christ, quarter to five," I shivered, although the November night was warm.

The front door was unlocked. We crept in.

"There it is," I pointed to a vinyl sofa in the hall, opposite the front door. We kissed.

"Sweet dreams," I whispered and tiptoed into my room.

"Where've you been?" Samuel demanded accusingly, as I sat down into bed.

"At the party. Raymond came back too; he's sleeping in the hall. He didn't have anywhere else to stay."

"I thought he left."

"Yeah, well, he came back." He put his arms around me.

"Night Roxy."

"Night."

Next day, I told Samuel what had happened. I wanted him to leave, so that I would be able to see Raymond openly without deception or betrayal.

"*What? WHO? When? Where? Why? How?*" Samuel's voice was shocked, disbelieving.

"At the party. After he came back. Look Samuel, remember we're not even supposed to be together now, are we? Remember that talk we had about commitment and babies, and I kept trying to get an answer from you, and you said you weren't ready for all that, and you didn't know if you ever would be?"

"So you slept with Raymond. Is he ready for that? You're crazy. Well if you slept with that dickhead, I'm going back to Canberra."

With gentlemanly controlled fury (and Samuel was ever the gentleman, gallant and faithful to his own idiosyncratic ethical code) he picked up Raymond's cassette player that was next to my turquoise portable typewriter, amidst the papers and books on my desk, and rushed out from the room. When he returned he seemed quite calm.

"Well," he said with quiet satisfaction. "I smashed Furnett's cassette player on the rocks."

I stared at him.

"What do you mean—smashed his cassette player?"

"I walked to the edge of the esplanade, dropped it on the rocks a few times then threw it into the sea."

"God, Samuel, how could you do that? Raymond lent it to us. It was very generous of him!!

"Yeah, well, too bad, it's gone now."

He smiled smugly, and lay down on the mattress, petulantly. His face had that proud, stubborn, obdurate and determined look, that I knew, and which meant this was going to be difficult. It would take all my strength to pull it off, to get him to leave, despite what he had said. I knew that I must keep quiet, and not talk to him. Samuel was a man of his word, with his own rigid sets of ethical rules he adhered to without compromise. Like doing one hundred push-ups a day and his kleptomaniac code. He would not go back on his word, unless I softened. I knew that if I looked at him with a slightest indication of relenting, relaxed a fraction, started talking; Samuel would, ignore my secret wishes, go back on his resolution. But if I kept up my resolute front he would feel compelled to go.

Our silent battle lasted a week. Every morning, I awoke with my will power strong as ever. All through the days and nights I constantly, silently, willed him to leave. I hardly dared breathe in case this gathering spell broke. I did this by focusing on my secret not-love, Raymond. I thought about him all the time. Inciting the moment I knew I must see him again.

After six days of stalemate, Samuel took out the panniers and slowly started to pack: his tee-shirts, spare pairs of jeans. His toothbrush. His towel. His top-quality English hairbrush. His camera. He left his top-of-the-range down-filled sleeping bag.

"You'll need it," he said, chivalrous to the end.

We were in my room. I was at my desk, reading.

"Roxy?" he said.

"Yes?"

"I didn't want to tell you at the time, because I didn't want to make you upset or scared. But now I'm going, I want you to know, just in case. Just in case anything happens, you'll be warned in advance. You can go to the police."

"What is it?" I stared at him.

"Before we left that house we stayed at. Frank pulled a gun on me. He said if I ever spoke to Cory again he was going to kill me and cut me up into pieces and bury me in the garden. He said he knew how to do it."

"WHAT!!!"

"I didn't want to scare you. That's why we had to leave so quickly. If he tries to contact you, call the police."

"What do you mean if he tries to contact me?"

"If you ever see him, and you feel threatened."

"How on earth would I ever see him?"

So much had happened since, it all seemed a long time ago.

It was in another part of town. It had nothing to do with me. Samuel was probably just saying that to try to get me back.

It was not enough to reignite our bond.

Ever since Samuel had committed the ultimate betrayal and slept with my sister, when we had been together a year, and then with his friend's girlfriend, and then with his brother's girlfriend—because he said he "needed" to have sexual experience—after I had overcome the initial devastating hurt, I had not found any good reason to remain loyal to him either. Ever since my treacherous sister had told me about how he seduced her when I was at my child-minding job, I had wanted to find someone I could have a faithful relationship with. If it was not for his disloyalty to me it could all be different now.

"Well, good-bye," he said when there was nothing else for him to do.

"Bye."

He gave me a big hug, endearingly awkward as a cartoon bear. He could hardly bend his elbows and move his arms, padded by his woolly jumper and his leather jacket. We'd been together four years and nine months. Since I was seventeen.

"Bye," I said again, I was deliberately modulating my tone of voice, keeping my physical expression neutral. I knew that Samuel was just longing now for the tiniest chink to show in my steel-plated armour, for me to smile at him, softly, warmly. It was extremely hard but I did not (dreaming of my not-love Raymond). I walked with Samuel out onto Rubicon Road. I stood on the pavement, as he put on his helmet, grasped onto the handlebars, slung his leg over the bike and sat down. He'd already attached the panniers. He looked at me, and I could see the tears in his eyes. "Bye Roxy." He pulled down his visor.

And then he raised his right leg, slammed his foot down on

the kick-starter, and he was off. Roaring down the quiet street in a burst of acceleration.

3

After Samuel left, I had lots of things to do. I had to finish a painting, a portrait of Margarita playing electric violin, and yellow commuters on Collins Street, in the city of Melbourne. I had to write an essay on Velázquez and the Baroque for Art History.

I walked over to the bottle shop in The Regal and bought a bottle of bubbly. I drank it slowly (toasting my triumph) as I worked on my portrait, then, I started to write: essay.

The reproduction of Velázquez's Maids of Honour is in black and white; its wash of greys is grainy. But its magic still shimmers through. The image, saturated with so many forms of light, dances into the eyes. Princess Margarita, with her long blonde hair, surrounded by playmates and maids. In front of her, are a dwarf and a large Flemish dog. To her left and right are two older girls, curtsying in a display of avid attendance. The group is standing in the artist's studio, where it is assumed, the text informs us, that the little princess has been posing for Velázquez. The artist has included himself in the portrait. He is a long haired, moustachioed figure dressed in the swashbuckling attire of the times, and holding a brush and palette. Standing before a canvas almost as tall as the high-ceilinged room. Its left edge is just visible on the left-hand side of the canvas, as if it is propped against and held up by the inside of the painting.
Two small figures are reflected in an illuminated mirror on the wall at the end of the room. The text reveals that they are the Infanta Margarita's royal parents, although it is hard to tell from the blurry indistinct image alone.

Whether the images are reflections of images Velázquez painted on his unseen canvas, or they are reflections of the 'real' couple standing out-of-frame in the space (where the viewer is positioned) to which the portrait group are all looking, as if towards the viewer who is, in turn, gazing into Velázquez's portrait, is also unclear and unknown.

Beside the mirror, in the vanishing point, is an open doorway in which a male figure is standing on stairs, which lead apparently into nowhere, but a rectangle of brilliant light. This figure also is turned towards the viewer. Although it was painted a couple of hundred years before the advent of photography, it looks as if all the figures in the group (except the reflected 'royal parents') are in the process of turning towards a photographer, who has captured them as they turn, before a formal pose has been struck. Velázquez opened a window onto a visible world created from light, challenging his viewers, in the process, to enter a labyrinth of reflections and optical tricks.

What at first sight looks to be a straightforward group portrait turns into a complex maze of shimmering mirage meaning...

I bashed out a few more lines on my portable typewriter, my most treasured possession.

> Cross the Rubicon
> and you will see
> a darker entrance
> to the sea
>
> a funfair waits
> on the other side
> you don't see the horror
> till you go on the ride

a creepy clown c
repeats d to infinity
you're on the way
when you say 'gee'

Where did the words come from? A surreal poem using a stream of consciousness I sometimes used when I wanted to write. I had no idea what it meant. The words had woken me up a few nights before.

I wondered when I'd see Raymond again.

Late next afternoon Raymond came to the house. Neither of us was on the phone so we had not been able to contact each other.

"Samuel's gone," I said.

We gazed into each other's eyes. Our lips met and it was as electric as the first time. I fell into his kisses, and it was like hurtling down the slide on the big dipper, I didn't want to stop falling. I wanted to fall like that, screaming and waving my arms in the air, forever. We went into my bedroom and made love on the mattress on the floor.

In the evening we wandered over to the bottle shop, Ray bought a bottle of South Australian Shiraz wine. We walked down to the beach, and lay on the warm sand. In front of us yachts anchored in the Bay bobbed on the water's surface. We drank the wine from plastic cups from the bottle shop. The wine stained Ray's lips black; I laughed, and he said it did the same to mine. In front of us, the sun slid into the sea, setting the yachts and the purple water alight.

"It's so romantic."

"Like being in the tunnel of love," I laughed.

"Instead of seeing a film we're looking at the real thing."

"Stretched out before us is an unrepeatable gift of nature: the evening sunset."

"You, me and the wine-dark sea..." Ray put his arm around my waist and pulled me closer to him.

"I want to drown with you..." I hoped it sounded ironic not cheesy.

The light faded and a huge December Rose Moon rose up from the rim of the ocean, rising high into the sky. When it was dark, the breeze off the Bay water freshened, and we returned to the house. I forgot about dinner, Ray didn't mention it. We made love on my mattress, and fell asleep in each other's arms.

"Don't die," said Raymond, one evening a few days later.

"What?"

"Now I've found you, I don't want to lose you. You'd better not die on me."

"I won't die! I'm here with you, for real," I laughed lightly. But it disturbed me; die figuratively, symbolically, or literally?

Where were his doubts coming from? Did I look unwell?

What was he talking about? I had no idea.

Ray drove me, in his parent's old car, to the university on the edge of the city, to drop off my last assignments and then it was over. I had completed First Year.

"Freedom!" I said, laughing, as we drove off. In my feverish projection, the prospect of an eternal enchanted summer was rolling out before us exorbitantly, shimmering, voluptuous, a gift of light and heat, not-love. It felt sensual, sensational, like the embodied Desire of a lover's mirage. A gift I could hardly bear was mine.

Rimbaud watched from the window as Verlaine ran out onto the street, blood was dripping from his hand...beside him a veiled belly dancer...and twenty camels, and Lawrence of Arabia who, before anyone noticed or could stop it from happening, had gone native in a turban and Bedouin robes...reclining on the hot sand beside his camel...

We ventured semi-dressed into the kitchen at Rubicon Road... The early summer night sang and shrieked with insect noise. We had been in the house alone, our palace of delights, and violent tender pleasures, and hadn't gone out for five days and nights.

Everyone had gone away, vanished on sudden vacations. In the end, the house of art students, which had begun with so much friendly promise, had disintegrated in animosity. At the end of first semester, Lily moved out after she left Ray, and after friction with Fraser. At the beginning of second semester, Margarita had moved out. Before he turned nasty, Fraser said that she'd "got into trouble" and had to have a termination. A succession of replacement lodgers took over Lily's room but they all proved to be unsatisfactory to Fraser. The leaseholder became vindictive—accusing everyone of extreme decadence, threatening retribution. But I didn't let that bother me.

Ray and I were the last ones left, survivors of a shipwreck, castaways on a desert island about to sink beneath the rising waves. The lease was about to end, and we had only a few days left. I hadn't made a decision about where to go. Mum's house, the Farm, Margarita's in Melbourne... I was just here, living in the moment, with Ray; the here and the now, that's all I was thinking of.

Living in my body. The universe condensed into a sigh, a shared inner world of feeling, the flicker of his eye; breathy tenor of his voice. As if in a dream, or poem, I mapped in my mind every mole and freckle on his pale skin. With my fingertips I traced the constellation of scars, the subtle language of his life's tattoos.

His frame was lighter than Sam's musclebound physique. The shape of Ray's bones under his skin, his wiriness, entranced me; he was not much taller than I.

I lost my appetite and he didn't seem to want to eat either.

As we stood in the kitchen, nibbling toast like penitents, Ray said, "I think I'll set out for Grafton in the next week or so, maybe hitch a ride in a truck. My cousin's place is about 40 k's from Grafton in mid-northern New South Wales, in the rainforest. He and Netta, his girlfriend, are living in what will one day be the barn, when they build a house. They built the barn by themselves, the shack where I'll be staying, and painting my works of genius is down the hill from their place. George might visit for a while. Do some *plein air* painting. It should be a blast, baby... do you still wanna come with me?"

His tone was hesitant.

A week? Ray had mentioned his plans before but I couldn't quite get my mind around it. George? He had so many painter friends, I lost track of who was who.

"Uh, yeah, okay, I think so," I said.

Ray had mentioned his cousin, Rex. As he described him, Rex grew into quite a wild man with an appetite for drinking and dope. Apparently he brewed his beer. Raymond had said that his cousin had consumed, in one binge, the produce of a whole "brewing kit" (many gallons) before the brewing time was up. I had laughed at his 'dramatic exaggeration for effect'.

Ray was good at that. Ray had told me he and Rex were both twenty-six. Their grandmother had 'brought up' and looked after both the cousins because their mothers went out to their full-time jobs. Whenever Ray had mentioned 'my cousin Rex' he had started laughing heartily as if they shared a secret bond that nobody else understood. But Raymond was not laughing now.

Ray's demeanour was serious; looking at me steadily, he was expecting an intelligent response. But I was having problems with the connection between my mind and my brain. The kind of mental experience that led eighteenth-century philosophers to question not only the verification principles/truth conditions of their existence, but those of the entire universe and its contents. My mind had gone blank. I couldn't visualize Rex, or Grafton, the rainforest or the shack. I could not think about my new love's plan.

The prospect of summer rippled through my thoughts like the vast expanse of beach beneath the blinding blue sky, the brilliant vista of the Bay, filled with light and yachts. Perhaps my projections had about as much substance as fairy-floss, but like a child at the fairground I didn't want the ride to end.

I was scared that making plans, particularly that involved other people, would end what we had between us, now, and explosively propel us into mundane duties of normal life that I wasn't ready to re-enter yet. I wanted us to stay as we were, enclosed in the private bubble of our (not) love, intense as the fated characters in that film *In the Realm of the Senses*—before she went mad and killed her lover and hacked off his penis. I didn't want to consider anything or anyone else but him.

"I've told my cousin that I'll probably be travelling with a Beautiful Lady," he coaxed, his hands lightly caressed my waist. He was looking at me very intently.

"That's you," he said. I loved his dry humour. His sophistication. But I had an uncertain feeling.

Although I didn't make a verbal reply, I made an effort to smile. We kissed again. I told myself that whatever happened, would be all right. That night, at the beginning of the year, on the beach, my lucky DNA star had promised. It would work out fine.

We awoke mid-morn. I got up and went to the bathroom, drank a glass of tap water, went back to bed. We made love on the mattress in burning beams of sunlight.

"You look like an angel," he said.

My eyes were semi-closed against the sun's rays slanting in sharp angles across the room.

Everything was white gold and radiant. He kneeled above me, haloed by the blinding luminescence pouring in through the window behind him. Caught in a sunbeam his arms, legs, torso, face illuminated to the point of disappearance. His hair glowed redder than mine.

"We recognized each other," he said.

Miraculously.

And then the doorbell started to ring.

"Just ignore it," I said. Someone kept ringing, and ringing, the bell.

"Someone is very persistent."

I stood up, swaying on the mattress.

"I'll just go and see who that is. Don't go away!"

I pulled on my yukata, wriggled my toes into a pair of flip-flops and, finger-combing my hair into place, I walked out of the bedroom, down the hall, and opened the front door.

Medusa

Surprise! "Surprise!"

Margarita. Standing on the doorstep. Suitcase in her hand. Her outfit was striking. Black and white checked gym-tunic. Zip-up ankle boots. Magenta lipstick. And a black straw hat, under which twitched a writhing nest of snakes.

A huge smile lit up her face.

"Sam said you've split up! He stayed over at my apartment, on the way through Melbourne. He was pretty upset. So you did it—well done, Roxy-baby!"

All I could do was gaze at Margy, in horror—those dreadlocks!—before quickly composing myself.

What was she doing here?

She pushed past me into the hall. I grabbed her arm and pulled her back.

"Did Sam mention that I'm with Raymond now?" I hissed in her ear.

"What?" Her expression of mischievous glee disappeared.

"No. He didn't mention it."

Her voice dropped a key. She stared at the floor, shoulders bowed, unguarded and deflated. Suddenly before me, I saw the image of a child whose present has been trashed. Although why I should feel guilty, I didn't know. More than anything I wanted to say: *Go Away!* But I couldn't do that. Margarita was my best friend.

"Uh, I'll just tell Raymond you're here. *He's been staying with me for a week, since Samuel left.*" I hissed the words with emphasis.

I stared at her, willing her to read my thoughts, guess that I am in not-love and it is bad timing and I wanted to be alone with him. I willed her to say that she would leave, and good luck with my new relationship. But she ignored my glare and meaningful emphasis, and didn't say anything.

She took a few more steps into the hallway brandishing her violin case.

"Uh, okay, hold on, I'll just go and get dressed," I said.

I hurried back into my room and closed the door behind me.

Ray was sitting on the bed. Looking at me expectantly.

"Margarita's here," I hissed, dropping my yukata over the back of a chair.

"What?" he looked puzzled.

"Margarita? Where did she come from?"

"She's come from Melbourne to stay. Samuel stayed at her place. He told her we've split up, and she's come here to stay with me. He didn't tell her about you and me. *She's got dreadlocks.*" I said sotto voce.

Ray looked bemused. He sat up, began to pull on his black pants.

I slipped into my black hipster skirt and purple vest from the pile of clothes flung over the chair at my worktable. After turning to smile at him again, I walked out of my bedroom.

I had to look after my friend. Make some tea, fix a bed; think about lunch. All the normal social things that I'd wanted to forget about for a bit longer.

"When did you decide to get the dreadlocks?" I asked as we sat around, sipping tea, in the kitchen.

"Oh!" she laughed. She reached up to her head, grabbed a few locks and started yanking and tugging at her own hair. I watched her in surprise, Ray watched her warily.

Suddenly she pulled even harder and scalped herself.

I stared at her blankly.

"It's a wig!" Margy cracked up in laughter. "A Medusa wig! I found it in a second hand theatrical shop." Her real hair was fastened with hairgrips. "I thought you'd like it! Oh God, the looks of yer faces be'jasus. I'm pissin' me sel'—" Exaggerating a mock Ballyweaver brogue for effect, as she did to amuse us all. Clutching her midriff, she ran from the kitchen, into the bathroom next door.

"Hmm!" said Ray. He picked up the wig, and put it on his head, cracked a wide grin, and started cackling with laughter; Margarita came back into the kitchen unpinning her natural locks.

"Shure, very fetching Furnett. Shure ye should wear yer hair in skinny wee bunches, like that, all the time, mon!" Her long glossy dark hair tumbled down over her face.

For the next five days, the three of us spent all our time together. Margarita came everywhere with Ray and I. On walks, to the shops… We went out to an opening at The Photographers' Gallery. And a party held by one of Ray's lecturers. Ray and I stopped walking to the beach in the evenings with bottles of wine. I didn't want to include her, nor to leave her out.

Almost every conversation I had with Ray, she was there—joining in. She wanted to talk with him about art, photography, music, people, films, books… anything. I started to think that *he* was her main attraction. My feelings of extreme desire for my new lover made me a little tongue-tied in his presence, even in intimate settings. Now Margarita was monopolizing every one of our getting-to-know-you conversations, in a way she never could have if it were Samuel. I thought that I could understand this, because of that. It was as if she was making up for lost time. After all those years I was with Samuel and she hardly got to open her mouth in his company...

I'd always felt a bit guilty that when Margarita came out from Northern Ireland and lived with the family, that I'd left home and was with Samuel. On the other hand it meant that she had a bed to sleep in, my old bunk bed in the room Lily and I had shared, and a space in my family that I had so unexpectedly 'vacated'. Margarita was my best friend at Ballyhope Grammar School, in County Antrim. We'd met, when we were both thirteen, a few months after the family moved from Bristol to Northern Ireland. I had been moved down a year to catch up on algebra, Pythagoras' theorem and the periodic table. She'd started coming home with me after school to The Old Parsonage The family had bought the three-storey Georgian mansion in the green fields of County Antrim. On a low rise overlooking a meandering river, it had a rhododendron drive, a field in the front and a stable-yard behind the house. We kept three ponies, a donkey, two goats, and thirty hens, our Labrador Dusty, cat Jester, and inherited black yard-cats. Margy also lived in the country in a heritage cloth mill mansion but unlike her family seat, Houndstooth Hall, that was a working farm, our house was heated and had carpet. For three years, as her family fended off bankruptcy, Margy practically lived with my family; she came on our family holidays to Europe. After we moved to Australia she'd worked as a waitress at a hotel in Portrush, to save up enough for the airfare to join us when she'd finished school.

With Margarita there, I was finding it hard to think about the summer, and making plans. The idea of going to Grafton with Ray was more difficult to think about. And what about George? I hadn't asked him about George yet. Who was he? Where did he fit into Ray's life?

And if I went to Grafton with Ray, what would Margarita do?

I'd had enough of thinking and talking; I brought out my palette and canvases and began to paint.

I painted three people; the three of us, on the porch of the house at Rubicon Road, three days after Margy arrived. Ray had made drinks. A cocktail he'd invented: vodka and blackberry nip. I painted him stockier than in reality. His image reflected in the Hall of Mirrors, grotesquely foreshortened. Dressed in black, hair crowning his head with a nimbus of spikes; natural pallor of his face. That was his performance art. Ray-Doe. Do ray mi, like the solfège scale, Dodo, the clown satirist of suburban life. Swinging the vodka bottle.

She, roaring with laughter, spitting a mouthful of vodka and blackberry nip, in a sparkling shining arc of light-filled droplets—right onto the top of my head.

She knew I was pissed off, as I jumped up and rushed into the house, but she didn't know quite how silently mad I was at her little joke, which they both seemed to find so funny.

It was one of those evenings; those long warm mauve-and-gold Adelaide December evenings, the air still fresh and clear before the onslaught of summer heat. The sky above filled with pink-gold clouds, a Renaissance vision of heaven; a sunset sky that, as its beauty becomes ever more intensely fleeting, looks as if it must go on forever.

The evening looked perfect, but it wasn't because my best friend was there. I couldn't ignore her, or forget her by losing myself, as I wanted to. Drinking with Ray in the vast luminescence, alone. Just the two of us not-lovers, taking off into inner space-lands together. I loved Ray, and drinking, but drinking with Ray was the *né-plus-ultra* definition of double-intoxication, divine, the hit amplified a million-fold because it was he, suburban escape artist *extraordinaire*. Already I was addicted to the heady cocktail of Ray-and-booze.

I could hardly attempt to disappear, take off into states of bliss with Ray now... What would be the point with Margarita there, just waiting for the chance to come and spit vodka and blackberry nip? And now it was all too late. It was all over. The lease was up and we had to leave.

I packed away the things in my room. Ray was living in his parents' garage. I couldn't stay with him there. I had decided to go with Margarita to Melbourne and then on to Canberra to Mum's house. Ray thought he'd visit me in Canberra, and I would then most likely travel on with him to Grafton and his cousin's place. I still hadn't asked him about George. I would ask him soon.

When I was immersed in the process of packing my things I found notes I'd written for my art history essay:

> *What characterizes paintings and sculptures of the Baroque era, as well as the presence of illumination, light—contrasted with shadow, darkness— was the aspect of what was left out, out-of-frame.*

I'd gazed at the reproduction and hadn't come any closer to solving the mysteries and paradoxes it set up.

I picked up a sheet of paper from the top of the pile on my desk. A fragment by a Russian poet who sought answers in music. She was left with the ghosts of memories, and silence. I read the words slowly. How beautiful.

I turned the page and found a few more lines.

The silence of your heart

Every night I dream of you
In my dreams I am
a million different people
not one of them can reach
the silence of your heart

I'd written this one night, using a technique of automatic writing surrealists used. The idea was to let the mind go and words flow. The words came from the subconscious which was supposed to be more intuitive, and authentic, if not visionary.

I slipped the lines between the pages of my notebook, and put it into my army bag with the precious notes I was saving for I didn't know what kind of posterity.

Then I picked up a piece of paper that I had written some notes on. It was a riddle. I had woken up one night with the words resounding through my mind. There was a high wind and the sound of the big wheel creaking woke me up, I think, or maybe it was the power of the words that woke me, telling me to write them down. But I did not know what it meant.

> a creepy clown c
> repeats d to infinity
> you're on the way
> when you say 'gee'

I folded it and put it into my army bag.

The day before we finally left the house a letter arrived to me addressed in Samuel's writing. I'd opened it to find a letter he'd written at Margarita's. He'd arrived at Margy's unannounced and she hadn't been there, he said. He wrote the letter to me over two days as he waited for her to return, feeling increasingly lonely and needing someone to talk to.

> Dear Roxy,
>
> I am sitting on Margy's big padded chair listening to Sticky Fingers, 'Wild Horses'; everything is fine except potato digger is nowhere to be found. I got here about eight o clock Sat night. Boy I wish you'd come; the coastline along the Great Ocean Road is absolutely stunning. A view from the Bay of Martyrs was so overwhelming, the feelings that it aroused in me were just

indescribable, such desolation—the fine salt spray—
miles of untouched coast—jutting headlands—penin-
sulas falling into the sea...

Margy still has not returned, the time being 1 p.m.
Sunday. Lucky I knew where she keeps the key. I'm
going to try and find the sea and go swimming and
walking. I shan't be staying long in Melbourne. I think
I might go to Selwyngrove, Edwin's friends' farm and
camp along the coast. Your the only girl for me darlin.

... It is very hot and I wish I was walking down
the beach and jumping off the Glenelg pier—diving
with you....This letter will probably go for some time
because I feel so lonely. I don't know how to get into
contact with Margy or Peter or any mutual friends. It
will be posted off tomorrow...

...I will be leaving Tuesday morning, come hell or
high water, I f***** well better see her before then. It
would be really good to talk to her. I've just remembered where Derrida's house is you know that party we
went to in Brunswick, upstairs, not his old house but
another one, well I think I remember something about
them moving in next door. I'm going to start to write
to Lily soon, it's rather selfish of me worrying about us
when she must be feeling so dreadful...

At the end of his letter were a few lines penned in a larger,
looser and equally familiar hand:

Well hi baby—the lost wanderer has at last
returned from a weekend in Prahran and a day at
the seaside only to find the Wolfe in me bed! What

a surprise-shure is grand to be seein the lad again. I hear yuz have been havin a wee separation for a while—a good idea I think but I bet your marbles it won't last long. My god today is so fucking hot. My pores feel as though they're full of cream and honey and fucking horrible. Anyway poppet how are you and whatever are you doing, I have been meaning always to visit in a couple of days or weeks but always something comes up, a job, music practice or an exam—always something to keep me here. But my plan, which I shall have to hurry cos Big Sam is itching to go and post this, is to come down next week-end and stay a week or so by the sea so what I shall do is wait until you send me your very prompt reply to say when you will depart Adelaide. I might even be able to come on Wed but then I'll wait till I hear from you cos Sam says it was in your wee head to leave on Friday for good and all [the first I had heard of it...].

So dwarling, write to tell me what you want to do—it would be nice to stay a week after exams should it not? Anyway write soon & tell me what you're doing—I'm not sure what I'm doing about moving, I'd like to move to the seaside, but the idea of shifting all my stuff does not exactly appeal.

I shall save all the gossip for when I see you in the near future.

So write immediately, priority paid & say the word—OK.

Hope you are in good shape.

All my love
    Marg xxxxxxx

Sorry for not having written

P.S. Big Sam is doing his pushups and nearly col-
lapsing with the effort

Reading these words produced a strange sensation of being caught in a time-space warp.

Instead of being 500 kilometres apart, as propriety dictated we should be, Margarita was chowing down on her breakfast fruit and yogurt but a few yards away from me in the living room. Well, it was too late to tell her not to come now.

"Guess what's just arrived?" I waved the missive aloft as I walked into the room where Margy was eating at the table.

"Oh, have you only just got it?" she said, looking shocked, and then starting to laugh.

"Next time send a telegram."

Heatwave

It was very hot in Melbourne. I'd been there a week with Margy, staying at her place in the inner city. Sleeping next to her, in her uncomfortable double bed. Under the corrugated-iron roof, the converted stable where she was living heated up like a toaster.

Raymond arrived in the dead of night. He'd written to me after I left. A postcard. He wanted to visit me in Melbourne; he said he couldn't wait until Canberra. I was sleeping, as too was Margy, but the banging on the door woke me. I jumped out of bed. I walked to the door and opened it, unbolting and swinging open the top half first, and then the bottom.

Ray was standing before me, an expression of shock on his face.

"Hi," I said.

He stared at me blankly without saying anything.

"Ray? Are you all right? Is there anything wrong?"

"Your kimono!" he said, without moving. I glanced down and saw it had come adrift, revealing my breasts.

"It's not a kimono it's a yukata! A lighter-weight garment that's less formal!"

I pulled the sides together, laughing, took Raymond's hand, guided him over the threshold and closed the stable doors. I placed the left-side panel of the yukata over the right. That was what I had learnt in Kyoto and not forgotten. 'Right-over-left' is how the dead are dressed in Japanese culture. When Margy wore the yukata I sent her for Christmas after the family had moved here, I was shocked to see that she was wearing it with the right-side panel placed over the left. I had omitted to tell her about that when I sent her the yukata from Kyoto. I hadn't wanted to tell her the real symbolic meaning, so I just said it was considered bad manners in Japan to wear it as she was. She had laughed, as if it didn't matter. I left a pamphlet with the information in it, as I did not want to break the bad news to her. But still she didn't care about the symbolic meaning, and wore it any way she wanted. She was wearing her yukata now as she slept.

I was amazed that Ray should care about seeing a glimpse of my skin. He was an artist!

I'd been to Back-To-Earth Festivals, where thousands of people congregated naked, swimming in the Cotter River, as a statement against the 'hypocrisy' of society; festivals which created alternatives, a market-economy of arts, wholefood, clothes, crafts, music. I had been to the festivals with friends from the alternative school. I had assumed everyone who was a freethinker and free spirit must be part of a naturist-friendly movement. A left-wing Labor deputy Prime Minister had founded the annual festival; many people believed an enlightened era was dawning, signified by a phrase such as 'back to earth'. My Grandmother was interested in this and wanted to hear me telling her about it on the phone, although Mum and Dad didn't approve of my going to the festivals, as they didn't approve of my going to the alternative school.

"So how are you?" I said.

"My head aches. I'm wrecked. I hitchhiked from Adelaide. Went to the truck stop outside Tailem Bend. Asked who was going to Melbourne, hitched a ride through. I've been sitting in a Mack truck for thirteen hours straight. The trucker gave me some of his wakey wakey pills they did my head in. I'm in another dimension. Lost a day or so it feels."

"Let me show you around Margarita's stable."

"The kitchen-dining-work room!" I gestured around me.

"The bedroom!" He followed me into the sleeping space. To save embarrassment, I pulled on a pair of pyjama trousers that I grabbed from a pile of clothes on the dressing table.

"Where'll I sleep?" he asked, looking bewildered.

"In the bed!" He looked even more puzzled.

"It's okay," I laughed. "I'll go in the middle. There's nowhere else to sleep, anyway, Ray. There's only one lot of bedding."

I jumped back in; he took off his clothes and joined me. He was wearing boxer shorts I noticed in amusement.

Margarita didn't wake up.

The heat wave hit next day. I awoke drenched in sweat. Above us the roof was creaking and cracking as the iron expanded in the soaring mid-morning temperature.

Ray pulled on his white jeans and Lone Deranger tee-shirt. I tied a short blue batik-patterned sarong around my hips and slipped into a purple vest and sun shirt. Margarita put on her black silk slip teamed flamboyantly with purple tights and tap dancing shoes. I watched in amusement, through the open stable doors, as she tapped in iambic pentameters across the flagstones to the bathroom in a wash shed in the centre of the former stable-yard. Margarita had not gone to the Back-to-Earth festivals, as she was in Northern Ireland then. By the time she came to Australia, punk had arrived. She'd picked up on it, in her own way, straight away.

"So, how's your work going?" I asked Ray, as we were sitting down to breakfast of fruit, yogurt and percolated coffee.

"Pretty good," he replied. "When I go back to Adelaide in two days I'll finish the Faces project, give it to the gallery, then leave. Set out for the rainforest. I'll come down, meet you here, or we can meet in Canberra, what do you think?"

I was not sure about going to the rainforest with Ray, and I was just about to say this, when Margarita butted in, as if he'd been talking to her.

"First I have to officially withdraw from my photography course," she said as she stood up, casually adjusting her purple stockings. Margarita appeared to be looking straight at Ray.

Her gesture was in the brazen spirit of the punk years that we all pretended we weren't embodying, and, as I'd felt several times since her unannounced arrival into my new relationship, I wasn't sure whether to be amused or annoyed.

"I'll do it this week, then I'll pack up all my stuff and move out of here," she said, airily.

Ray was gazing at her with an inscrutable look.

"It's okay to leave it at your Mum's, isn't it?" She looked at me.

"Yeah," I said without enthusiasm, wishing that I was going back to Adelaide with Ray, which I couldn't do as he was still living in his parent's garage. He'd said that they would not approve of my joining him in his homeless hideaway. I knew what it was like, as I had visited him there with Samuel one time, when Ray was ill. Ray had a single mattress on the bare concrete floor, flanked by worn-out white-goods, faded old furniture, and the family car, an ageing Valiant. So, instead, I had to stay here, in limbo, with Margarita in her stable.

Languid in the heat, I dreamily watched her apply make-up. Squinting at her reflection in a shaving mirror on the kitchen table, head tilted backwards, exposing the curve of her throat; she outlined her eyes with kohl. Stretching the eyelid out with her fingers. With deft flicks of her powder puff, she fluffed her cheeks and nose, absorbing a layer of whitish sunscreen-shine. She painted a magenta lipstick smile. She studied her handi-work, briskly zipped up her black and white striped cosmetic bag, and popped it into her handbag. In the construction of her personae, like so many of our acquaintances, Margy com-bined the theatricality of a fairground sideshow actor with the precision of a high wire circus performer. With gusto, increas-ing numbers of our generation were tuning into a new way of being, and dressing.

She smacked her lips noisily, in exaggerated air-kisses.

"Okay Darlings!" she trilled. "I'm going to go out now. Got to see Derrida about some busking. I'll be back this afternoon! Be good, poppets!"

Picking up parasol and bag, she clattered across the yard in her black tap shoes. Ray watched her in bemusement. Mum's black silk slip shone, glossy and sleek.

"*Nevermore,*" I thought. If Margy were a bird, no contest, she'd be a raven.

As soon the rhythmic clatter of her tap shoes receded into the distance, Ray and I jumped back onto the bed. It was too hot to sit in the kitchen. The temperature reminded me of the first time we made love. It seemed a long time ago.

"Do you remember that little room?" I said. I'd wanted to believe that my feelings for Ray were becoming more intense, crystalline, the longer I was with him.

Ray said he wanted to go to the National Gallery of Victoria to see *Untitled* a conceptual exhibition by Fan D'lavin, as did I. We set off at mid-day. It was like walking out into a metallic city. As if Melbourne had been transformed into a different set of elements overnight as we slept. Silver, copper, platinum, white gold laser-rays hit us from all angles. The houses, shops, roads, fences, cars, shone as if refracting blinding fluorescent rays in the dazzling alchemical light, the inhuman heat.

"Oh no, John Lennon's been shot!" I exclaimed in shock as I read the headlines on a sandwich board outside a newsagent.

Not realising it was commemorative, out of date. "Whoa," said Ray, looking stunned.

There were few people out. The streets, even in this usually busy inner city suburb were deserted. The city was becalmed, immobilized at 48 degrees Celsius. In Glenelg when it was very hot, gazing at the Bay had made me think of Coleridge's *Rime of the Ancyent Marinere*. The stationary yachts stuck in the still glittering seascape like painted ships upon a painted ocean evoked a terrifying solipsistic universe. Alone with one's thoughts, meaningful communication was impossible. That was before my relationship with Ray.

I remembered, in a café, I had read an article in the *Adelaide Argus*. A journalist was putting forth a theory about missing children in Adelaide who'd never been found, the story was in newspapers a lot I'd noticed, when I read the papers in cafés: suggesting they could have been taken out to a yacht in the marina. There were so many boats they could not all be seen from the shore. I had suddenly felt as if I was fainting. It happened to me when I read about horrific things. It was called 'vasovagal syndrome' a doctor had told me.

As we walked down the hill, towards the city, we passed a couple of middle-aged women leaning on fences, holding onto the metal bars like swimmers in trouble clutching onto buoys, faces grey and clammy with sweat. They looked faint.

We walked into a corner-shop.

JOHN LENNON SHOT

The headline was emblazoned on rows of front pages. The two Greek guys behind the counter, with dazed looks, handed us the wrong change for the bottles of water we bought; we realized later, walking down the street. It felt like a ghost town. But there was a weird sense of expectation in the shimmering too-hot stillness. As if, having exceeded all reasonable limits of temperature, anything else could now happen...

As if, at any moment, the city could be looted, pillaged by gangs of lawless marauders, because everyone has heat exhaustion.

Fireballs could spontaneously combust in the bursting air and go bowling down the street. Time could go backwards...

The gallery was air-conditioned; we stayed there for hours.

We returned to Margarita's stable in the early evening with a bottle of red wine. She was not there. The stable was stifling, airless. It was too hot to cook anything; we made a salad, with bread, and cheese we found in the fridge.

"Why don't we go and sit in the park down the road," said Ray after we'd finished eating. He was referring to a small grassy area with bushes, on a traffic island in the middle of the road. It would never have occurred to me to go there. But it was in a back street and very quiet.

"Let's take a blanket to lie on," he said.

I laughed. I thought he was joking.

But Ray said: "It's the thing to do. Like sleeping outdoors in the garden when you're a kid in summer, or setting up for a picnic. Bring the wine and a couple of glasses."

"All these Australian traditions I'm finding out about," I replied.

We reclined languidly on the blanket, drank the wine, and rolled over onto our backs staring up at a thick layer of smog, trying to detect a few stars.

Next morning, Margarita was still not back, and the temperature was, if possible, even higher.

"Let's go to St Kilda. Have a swim. Cool down," I suggested.

"Yup. Sounds good," Ray replied.

We caught a tram there. When we arrived at the seafront, we found much of the fit population of Melbourne had been struck by the same idea. The beach was blanketed with a shiny layer of comatose bodies, stretched out on towels on the sand, basting beneath the blazing sun. Acres of red-brown flesh covered in oils and lotions, sizzling and steaming tenderly. The sea was full of bodies, but everyone seemed to be standing still, splashing feebly. It was too hot to move. We sought shelter in a large covered pavilion that looked shady, but inside was hot as the beach. I was wearing a sarong and black vest under a purple silk sun-shirt. I took off the sarong and shirt. (I hadn't worn swimmers or a bikini since I threw out my make-up and high heels and went back to earth a few years ago).

"I'm not going in, sport, I'm going to stay here," said Ray, his face bright pink, glistening with perspiration. He sat down and pulled out his visual diary from his backpack. The sand was burning hot. I had to run across it to try to prevent the soles of my feet from being fried. The water when I reached it was glassy and torpid, like opaque yellow-green jelly before it's quite set, or, more prosaically, bath water that's been urinated in. I stayed in for about ten minutes, diving under, hoping to cool down. But the water was almost as hot as the air.

"Let's find a pub," Ray said, when I returned.

"Good idea."

The pub was cool, air conditioned, and we stayed there for hours. I sipped beer, sitting close to Ray sipping beer, in front of us large tinted windows, we gazed.

Margarita was back, in her stable, when we returned. Buzzing around, laughing and talking at high speed, totally refreshed.

"I went to a nightclub on the roof at the Archangel Hotel, after seeing Derrida. I met a chap, Scotch College-educated, very good looking, who invited me over to his parents' house. His parents were away; their *mansion,* in Toorak, had a huge swimming pool. I've just endured a couple of days lounging around the pool, suffering having cocktails brought out to me by gorgeous young men..."

I stared at her in disgust.

"God. And I was worried something *bad* had happened to you. We've hardly been able to move in this heat."

"I was talking about Adelaide, and mentioned staying at your house opposite the funfair, and George said he thought he might know someone who lived there. He used to live with him in a group house in Melbourne; he was studying architecture at Commerce University. But then he had a motorbike accident and had to go back to Adelaide where he grew up. I think it could have been your man Fraser."

"Maybe. You know he became somewhat deranged before we left. It wasn't good, actually. It was terrible. After Margarita and Lily left. He became really paranoid and aggressive. That's a coincidence."

"Yeah, small world."

"Are you going to see your young chap again?"

"No," she said, tossing back her dreadlocks.

I saw what I interpreted as a "split-second" look, an involuntary expression of pain and jealousy, as she glanced at Ray then me. Then she turned and tap danced out of her bedroom, toes and heels clacking on the worn linoleum. It was only later that I realized she had mentioned a 'George,' which reminded me that I still hadn't asked Ray about the George who might be visiting him in the forest when I was there, if I went.

We had one day left. Then Ray was returning to Adelaide, to sign a form. Margarita and I were going to take the train to Canberra. We were going to stay at my mother's house over Christmas (although we'd all but stopped celebrating it). I asked her what she thought about whether or not I should go to the rainforest, when Ray went out to the shops for milk.

"It's your decision," she said. Then she hurried out. I heard her crossing the cobbled yard. There was certainly something upsetting her.

On Ray's last night in Melbourne the three of us went out to Ronny's Green Room, a local pool hall and bar that Margy found. We ordered drinks, and sat in the green-lit darkness near the bar. Margarita seemed refreshed and full of energy. I was sunburnt and dazed by the heat. Although I was sitting opposite her at the table with Ray, I felt like a person in the audience watching a diva's exaggerated theatrical performance. In hidden irritation, I marvelled at her black-and-purple velvet bodice with plunging neckline, her magenta lipstick, and her dreadlocks. Her soprano laughter could have shattered glass. I felt a headache coming on.

I shifted my gaze to the rectangle of smoky green light, to the pool-room visible through a doorway. I could see the dim shapes of players moving slowly, circling pool sharks.

In my line of sight, on the next table was an old newspaper. My eyes were drawn to the headline.

15 YEARS SINCE THE CHILDREN WENT MISSING ON GLENELG BEACH

Glenelg Beach? I leaned over and picked up the paper.

On Australia Day 1966, three siblings aged 9, 7, and 4, went to play on their local beach and were given a curfew of 3 p.m. Their parents said the children always came home on time. But that day was different. It was to become known as the day that Australia lost its innocence, the day that three children disappeared, that was to change the way that parents in Australia supervised their children, forever.

The children vanished and are thought to have been murdered. The last person to give a sighting of the siblings was a shopkeeper who saw the three on Jetty Road in the company of a young adult male.

Some experts have put forward the idea that the children could have been smuggled onto a boat. It was Australia Day and there were many yachts on the water. This might account for the mystery that no trace of them has ever been found. They could have been taken away onto a yacht and their bodies disposed of. Another murder scenario experts have suggested concerns waste water drains that flow out offshore.

There are new speculations of connections to the abductions of young people, and the disappearances of children in Adelaide since then. Are there connections to the abductions and horrific murders of young men? There have been more reports that young men are being lured or dragged into cars and they are then being drugged and murdered.

The Editor, Australia Day, January 26, 1981

I was horribly chilled by the speculations, I felt queasy and turned the page.

Words

Kambah

HA! I made it, more or less. There were quite a few too many people on the train, (more than two), but managed to score a double seat to myself at NHILL and drift off into a state of semi-consciousness. Dreamt of you—ahhhh! Leaving was to say the least unpleasant. It was excruciating—as in not good. I hope we don't make a habit of it, eh. No doubt you feel much the same (I hope).

Returning to the house in Canberra was always uncomfortably pleasant. Not too bad for the first hour or so as I tried to pretend, but then, as I remembered that I'd never felt at home here, the anxiety set in with a vengeance, overcoming my claustrophobic desires to go into the kitchen and gorge myself with ice cream and nuts from the food cupboard.

We'd been at Mum's house for five days. That morning, I left the house to go to the shops to get a carton of milk for coffee. On my way out to Boswell Circuit, at the top of the driveway, I passed the mailbox. A distinctive bulging white envelope was wedged with a bunch of other mail sticking out from the wooden box. We'd spent intense days in Melbourne. As we'd said good-bye at Collins Street Station, he said he'd write, but I hadn't known whether to believe him.

I extracted the letter from the rest of the mail. My name was written on the envelope, c/-o Mum's address, in handwriting that was large cursive, erratic, and transmitted in blue biro. As I stared at the address on the envelope, I realized that I didn't know what his handwriting looked like. I'd only ever seen his writing on the very short printed postcard he'd sent to Melbourne, and the card he'd made me for my twenty-first birthday, on which he'd written *Happy Fucking B/day.* For my birthday my housemates had made a surprise birthday dinner for me, and organised entertainment: going out to see a band in the city. I had kept his card in my bedroom, on the mantelpiece over the fireplace and when the police came to search the house (after Lily and Margarita left), as Fraser had became paranoid, and told them something about drugs in the house, though I never knew what he said, trying to get me into trouble, an officer picked up the card, and asked: "Who's this from?" "A friend." "Nice friends," the police officer said. Yes, I thought, thanks Fraser, very nice.

I did not think about it afterwards. I dismissed it as ridiculous. It did not occur to me there would be a record and that it could affect me in the future. Even though it was a malicious lie, and there was no evidence to support what he said. I never took drugs and there were none.

I looked at the envelope. DOE, the name of Ray's alter ego was inscribed on the back. I forgot all about milk, and coffee. I stood by the wooden mailbox at the top of the driveway in the full-on glare of the sun, examining his writing style on the envelope and his choice of stamp.

All I could think was: I had to read it. Now. I walked back into the house. Margarita was in Alex's old room, practicing the same piece by Bach, the Fugue in D, over and over again.

It sounded to me like the sound of writing lines in detention, an exercise I had become well acquainted with in the grand days of Ballyhope Grammar. Alex had left home and Margy was staying in his old room. It had a piano. In Mum's house, another side of Margarita came into display. She helped with the washing up, and swept the floors. She laughed and joked, socializing with Mum. She wore her black silk slip, her hair loose and natural; and she practiced piano non-stop as if she had to give her hands something to do.

I took the letter outside onto the front porch (no one ever called it the veranda), where I thought I had the best chance of being undisturbed. I sat in the shade with a scenic view of the next-door neighbour's yard, fenced with a wee bit of string that he'd tied to long stakes pegged into the ground, to try to stop people from walking in a straight line across the communal grasslands to the embankment and highway, up and down which vehicles were moving through the morning heat. Instead of going around we walked over it; Lily used to step on the string and trample it into the ground.

I slit open the envelope with my fingernails and pulled out a fat bundle of papers that looked like they'd been ripped from a notebook. I unfolded and read ten pages of his words:

> ...Feeling depressed, at present sometimes the urge to hold you is desperate...
>
> ...At times I, when thinking of you, it would almost tear me apart, jump off the train to drag myself back. Just to look at you, feel you breathing as I held you. Leaving, wow, as you would say wasn't good. In Melbourne I was with you for a few days anyway—it broke up the time that we will be apart—it would definitely have

been too long for me.....Feeling very quiet and meditative. Living within the moments we have spent together. Dreaming of lying with you, our last time at the park or walks and wine on the Glenelg Esplanade, dawn in your bedroom, or you looking pissed off in what's his name's green slime room. Blackberry nip and vodka up your nose Margy out of it slurring apologies. I remember a great deal of detail of our times together—they and possibility of more are what sustain me in this dull parish...

Suddenly I longed to see him, to be with him again. I missed his voice in my ear telling me all about his art, his ideas.

> Languishing in your company, a caress, ecstasy, soft kisses ahhhhh! O to actually touch you, be with you, and hold you once again. The things I have from Melbourne, it's like waking from a dream, holding objects that were in that dream...
> Our experiences have been committed to eternity – nothing can touch our past.
> Love Raymond   I wish I was there with this to hug you!

I couldn't stop thinking about him, wanting him back again.

That evening, when Mum returned from her day's work with the Health Department, I broached the subject of Ray coming to stay at Kambah.

"Just for a couple of nights, on his way through to Grafton. He's a friend from Adelaide, a student," I said.

"Well... Yes, I suppose so," she said, her expression tight-lipped and disapproving.

I didn't say so, but I was silently overjoyed, surprised, and grateful that she didn't refuse outright to let him stay.

On a hot afternoon in January, Ray arrived at Mum's house in Kambah. He walked up the driveway and through the garden to the back door. As I washed a cup at the sink, through the kitchen window, I watched him cross the yard. I dried my hands and went to meet him as he walked up the concrete steps to the back door.

"Welcome to our palatial home," I said as he smiled at me and reached out and touched my arm.

"It's you!" he said.

I smiled back and we kissed on the lips.

"It's this way, in here, through the laundry," I said.

The laundry/back porch had room enough for one person; the two dogs, a German Shepherd and an Irish Setter, slept in there at night covering the entire floor.

I might have felt more uncomfortable about the starkness of Mum's house and lack of vegetation surrounding it despite the efforts she had made to nurture a garden if I hadn't been to Ray's family's place when he was sleeping in their garage. Ray's family's house was an equally unprepossessing bungalow, although not new. It was very different to the house Samuel's mother and stepfather lived in: the former embassy of a south east Asian country we no longer had diplomatic ties with, set in sweeping, leafy, established gardens in what was known as the 'diplomatic suburb', next to the lake. Samuel and I had stayed there in his bedroom in 'the boy's part of the house'.

"Where can I put this," Ray said, holding up a cardboard tray of beer. "I brought a slab," he laughed with the cackling tone of his social—or perhaps more accurately anti-social—laugh.

"A slab?" Margarita's voice rang out, as she walked into the kitchen. "Do you mean ye've brought a slab of cake, have yer, Furnett!" she said in a broad Ballyweaver brogue. "Sure is it a chocolate or plain sponge cake ye have with ye there, boyo?"

Ray laughed again, a softer tone. I noticed his face had a slightly shy expression of mild bemusement.

"Hello Margy," he said.

"I'll get glasses." I suddenly very much felt like a drink.

"I never drink beer, a change is as good as a holiday..."

Ray, Margarita and I sat on the front porch, drinking beer, chatting, idly watching the cars intermittently moving along the highway on the embankment fifty metres in front of us. The actual highway was out of sight, all that could be seen was the grassy slope of the embankment and atop it moving traffic; this produced a flat one-dimensional surrealistic effect. Adding to the stark atmosphere: a tall, spindly, lighting pole at the top of a steep flight of concrete steps that led up and down to the highway, a few strategically placed telegraph poles and sodium lamps sticking up from the edges of the implied road. I'd drawn this view many times over the five years since the family had moved to this house: stark line drawings in purple and black, which I'd composed before I left home in the afternoons or evenings or the solitude of the front porch at night and later from my memory. Margarita and I poured the beer from the cans into crystal glasses which we drank from. Ray drank directly from aluminium cans. Nick Cave was intoning on the stereo in the living room behind us. After a couple of hours, I heard the back door open and close.

"It's Mum." I said, *sotto voce*. The music suddenly dropped several decibels. Margy avoided my eyes.

I could hear the sound of Mum's heels, advancing loudly, as she walked through the living room behind us.

"Hi Isobel," said Margarita brightly.

"Hello Margarita. Hello Roxanne— "

"Hi Mum," I said, as I turned towards my mother standing in the doorway. She looked smart and distant, in a pink and olive summer suit, dark hair twirled up in a chic chignon, her face powdered, made up.

"G'day—I'm Ray," Ray said with a manic laugh.

"Mum. This is Raymond. Umm—He's an artist," I said.

"Hello *Ray*mond," said Mum with a disapproving emphasis on his name that made my toes curl. He was sitting on Grandmother's colonial chair at Grandmother's rattan table, in his white jeans, wearing his Lone Deranger tee-shirt and big black paint-spattered leather boots. The backpack in which he kept his art equipment was by his side. She averted her eyes.

"Could *you* help me, Margarita," she said, turning to my friend. "I need *someone* to help me unload the car. It's full of Cancer Foundation materials that I need to use for a shopping mall display."

"Yes, of course," Margarita said, as if Mum had just made a value judgement and she was agreeing with her. She jumped and followed her inside.

After all the beer was finished, Ray went to the bottle shop to buy some more. Margy said goodnight. She said she thought she might be getting a migraine; and she had to get up early as she was getting a lift with Mum to the shopping mall to post a late Christmas parcel to Northern Ireland. Ray and I stayed up on the porch for another hour. Ray was full of talk about the ceramic works that he planned to make at Styx Crossing, where he was going to stay in his cousin's shed.

"I'm going to work with forms. Raw, distinctive, studies of the landscape: voluptuous, and fleshy. I'm going to make them bisexual, not recognizably male or female, just human, yet appealing to the sensuous nature of both…forms that are about to burst or float away, very rounded buoyant forms, very simple lines, the glazing should follow," he said.

"I'm going to open fire it," he added.

"That sounds good," I said.

"What colours would you use?"

"Shades of red, blue, yellow. Primary colours."

Ray slept in the bunks in my old room, rather than sleeping in the top alone, we both slept in the bottom bunk. Mum and Margy had left by the time we woke up.

"Your mother's an attractive woman," Ray said as we were making breakfast. "I don't know why your father left her."

"Who knows how these things happen?" I felt irritated — was it really his business?—gazing through the window at the Brindabellas shimmering in the distance. It was after 11.00 a.m. and the mountains were rippling in the heat, dissolving in translucent tissue layers of blue and mauve colour and light.

We ate our breakfast on the front porch, as we talked about the perennial topic: what we were going to do.

"And what about the baggage? What's she going to do over the summer?" Ray said.

"Baggage??"

"Yeah, what's her face, Margy? Your satellite personality."

"Margy's not baggage! You can't call her that."

"Well she's hanging around you like baggage."

"No she's not, Margy's lived with us ever since just after I first met her in Northern Ireland, she's lived with our family.

"She doesn't seem to have her own life, or know what to do?"

"She's just trying to decide what to do at the moment," I said patiently.

"She's not sure what course she should take. Photography or Classical Music. That's okay."

Late afternoon. Thursday. January. Lying on my bed. Everyone is out somewhere. Why does his approval of my mother feel like a betrayal of me? The old feeling of restlessness is coming back with a vengeance. I feel like I'm in a trap. All I want to do is go, flee, escape, and get out. Have decided I will go to Greek Islands; travel round Europe, as I have been thinking of. Have been trying to persuade Ray to accompany me. He says he's not ready for a trip like that. He says: "I can do all the travelling I want in my own kitchen"…

A sudden burst of soprano laughter floated through the window, Margarita's high-pitched voice. Followed by Ray's deeper cackle. It sounded like they were on the front porch (no one ever called it simply 'the porch'). She'd said she was going to be practicing. I thought she meant her violin.

I threw my notebook into my airline bag and moseyed out. Ray and Margarita were sitting drinking beer in the shade of the front porch.

"Have a Bitter Drop," Ray said. He picked out a can from the six-pack by his boots and passed it to me.

Margarita was gazing at the marigolds, a studious expression on her face. As I watched her, her lips started quivering suspiciously.

Suddenly she jumped out of her chair and rushed indoors.

As she crossed the threshold she exploded with laughter.

A couple of minutes later the squeaky sounds of her violin tuning up rent the hot dry air.

"What's up with her?"

"She's a nutter," Ray said.

How odd, I thought. Since we first met at school in N.I., Margarita had always been known in the context of my family as practical, down-to-earth, the sensible one in the terrible trio of Margy, Lily and I. But even I had to admit, as her best friend, that Margarita had been behaving rather strangely lately.

"It's ever since she moved to Melbourne. It's affected her in strange ways. Or maybe it's the heat. We're all going troppo in Tuggeranong."

One night Ray and I went to The Bar to see Double Negation, Carl's manically visionary punk band. Margy didn't feel like going. Carl, the lead singer was a 'close acquaintance' from a long way back.

After the show I took Ray backstage to meet him.

"We're going to a party, do you want to come?" said Carl staring at my face intently. His large eyes were blue, penetrating beneath heavy lids. He was gazing at me with a glassy, fixed stare, as if he were in the process of being hypnotized. Carl always did like to act out a performance of slavish adoration.

I'd first met Carl two years before when Samuel and I were living in a shared 'group house' in Canberra with friends from the alternative school I'd gone to where I met Samuel (actually, I had first met Sam at his family's house with Dad, a colleague of Samuel's step-father, years before). The band Beno joined had practiced in the large garage under the house. Carl would come into the kitchen with the rest of the guys in the band, and he would stare at me across the kitchen as I made a plate of cheese-and-tomato-on-crispbread, which I carried back to Samuel in our shared room. The way he stared at me it was as if he had never seen anyone prepare a snack in his entire life. Carl was five years older than me and had studied History at university before dropping out. He seemed to know a lot about edgy literature, underground music that he called "intense"; and he, by chance, introduced me to Rimbaud. Occasionally, Samuel would take motorbike trips alone. One time, there was a party in the house and, for hours, Carl read to me from his book by Rimbaud, in Samuel's and my bedroom until the night sky grew light.

Then Carl had moved to Sydney with his band and released a vinyl album of songs of unrequited love that became quite a hit on the underground scene.

"Okay, I'll go," I said, glancing at him. But as we headed outside to the band's vehicles, Ray turned to me...

"You go sport, I'll head back to the ranch."

"Are you sure?"

"Yeah."

"Well, okay then. Bye."

Ray walked away across the car park. I followed Carl to the van where the roadie guys were loading up the equipment.

At the party, I talked all the time to Carl. I was vaguely aware of volleys of hostile looks being fired at me, by a bevy of scantily clad, heavily made-up, chain-smoking girls who had come from Sydney with the band.

Carl suggested I stay the night with him at the house of a friend of his.

"Okay," I said. "Because it's late."

We lay next to each other under a blanket on the carpeted living room floor at the house of his friend who disappeared back into the house, after opening the front door and showing us the living room. I kept my old army trousers and vest on.

"I love you, you know," Carl whispered, running his fingers through my hair. I turned my face away, as he tried to kiss me, and he sighed soulfully, a great show of unrequited devotion.

Neither of us mentioned our encounter in Adelaide. But it was odd. Why had he visited me there? It did not occur to me there could be sinister motives underlying his well-known 'intense' and unreciprocated love for me. Hence enabling him to keep a distance, yet to keep me in his sights.

Next morning I arose early and quickly, still fully dressed. I went to the bathroom, splashed warm water on my face and smoothed my hair.

"Well I'm going," I said, as Carl was folding the blanket. "Sayonara."

"See you in another life. Take it very easy," Carl murmured as we parted on the doorstep.

Kambah was a few suburbs yonder. I walked a kilometre, caught a bus down the Tuggeranong Parkway, then turned left and walked up the gravelly shoulder of the highway. Then I cantered sideways, down the steep grassy embankment, across the grass in front of the neighbouring house, to Mum's. Instead of walking up onto the front porch and knocking on the front door, I opened the side gate and went through the backyard, around the house, up the concrete steps to the back door, into the small laundry, pushing aside the dogs, who were jumping up and slathering all over me. It was two paces into the small kitchen area. I entered the kitchen surrounded by the excited dogs. Margarita and Ray were standing there, talking. Margy was making tea. Ray looked at me and I looked at him.

"Have fun?" he said.

"I had to stay over, I had no way of getting home," I said.

Margy and Ray had the air of interlocutors in the depths of a thoroughly absorbing conversation.

Margarita continued excitedly:

"Remix music is very neo-baroque, electronic remixing and sampling use very similar techniques to those that Bach used in *The Art of Fugue* creating an endlessly looping, polyphonic composition in the structure of the round, if the composer didn't decide to bring the piece an end it could go on for ever, repeating to infinity..."

"I'm going to have a shower, chaps," I said picking up a cup of tea from the bench and walking out of the kitchen. Neither of them acknowledged my announcement.

My correspondence with Dad had resumed after I started studying at university. He'd been sending letters, and letting me know what he was doing. He and his girlfriend had moved from their first rented flat to a rented house in an older suburb of inner Canberra. I'd visited them once at the start of the summer. Dad said they were going overseas for his work for three weeks and that I could stay there while they were away if I liked. Most of the time Margy and I stayed at Mum's. I usually kept quite a wide berth from Dad and his girlfriend. But when Raymond visited and the tension was escalating, I decided that Ray and I could stay at Dad's place, which we did for two days. But I had mistaken their return date.

One afternoon as Ray and I were lounging around, talking,

I heard the familiar tones of my father's voice and footsteps approaching the house.

"They're back! Quick! Get dressed!" We were lying on the couch.

I jumped up, raced into their bedroom, pulled on my dress, which was lying in a heap on the floor, frantically made their bed, pulling up the duvet and smoothing the pillows.

I finger combed my hair as Ray scrambled into his white jeans and black tee-shirt; luckily he wasn't wearing his Lone Deranger classic.

This was all achieved in a mad adrenalin burst of less than three minutes as they paid the taxi driver, brought their bags to the front door, put the key in the lock and turned it.

"What's that?" I heard my father say.

"Well...It looks like someone's here." She said, sounding calmly mystified.

"Hi Dad! Hi Dee!" I said confidently, as I strode into their living room where they were standing, gazing in surprise at me and Raymond who was following me.

"This is Raymond—he's a friend from Adelaide. He's an artist!"

"Hello, Raymond." Dad was smiling urbanely.

"Oh. Hi Roxanne. Raymond." Dee looked rather put out, for a moment, unlike Dad.

"Well. I'll just go and put the kettle on." She said, hurrying into the kitchen.

We chatted about where they'd been, their garden, which I'd watered, and Dad asked Ray about art.

We left on friendly terms. I was astounded and relieved that they had seemed so urbane and accepting and that Dad had seemed to be interested in Raymond and what he was doing and to like him. It was on the level of sociability. Staying there had been like being in an oasis of calm; and gave Raymond and I the chance to get to know each other a little better. We returned to Mum's crowded house in Kambah and the chaotic dance of all our interacting steps resumed its frantic pace.

Ray stayed another three nights. We went on long walks from the house, down the dirt track that skirted the blocks of brand new houses. To and from the agistment paddocks at a farm a couple of kilometres away to where Selena, my Anglo-Arab brood mare, lived with colt, Casper. We'd bought Selena from an Arabian horse stud fifty kilometres west of Canberra after seeing an advertisement in *The Canberra Chronicle*: 'Anglo-Arab mare in foal to pure Arabian.' The asking price was low compared to prices in Ireland or England. It seemed like buying two Arabs for the price of an old nag back home, we had decided. Selena, a 15.2 grey, had been the riding horse of the station manager. She had a beautiful disposition and temperament. When we'd bought her in foal the family planned to have the foal broken in as a riding horse to replace our horses in Northern Ireland. Then I'd left home, followed by Dad, and Lily and Alex—leaving my youngest sister, twelve-year-old Sarah, with Mum. After that, nobody discussed what we should do with the horses. When I stayed at the house I always took the dogs on walks 'down to see the horses'.

Ray and I walked to the horses, in the middle of his last day. It was extremely hot, the dry air burning against my skin. We had long, confused, tangled conversations, but it all collapsed into incoherence and we ended up getting nowhere. I couldn't make up my mind if I wanted to be with him or not. As soon as I decided I didn't, I immediately wanted him. And then I thought I shouldn't, so tried not to again. Decided I didn't and then I did. And didn't and did…Then didn't and did, and didn't, did, DID… And so it went on: an endless circle, the point of which I couldn't grasp. On our last walk 'to see the horses,' Ray explained—for the nth time—that he was going north to stay at his cousin's place in the rainforest. He invited me, again, to go with him. I said, "I'm not ready to go yet."

With Ray gone to Grafton, things settled down a little in the house. The atmosphere of violent tension and confusion, the dangerous energy abated. Mum and Margarita relaxed. Margarita was spending most of her time in Alex's old bedroom playing either the piano or her violin. Mum was spending all her time at her work, with the Health Department. I worked in Lily's and my old bedroom, painting and writing. I couldn't think about Ray or how I felt about him. If I tried to, my mind clouded, thick mental fog, visibility reduced to zero.

Days passed. Time enough to have gotten over it, I thought. The letter was slim; I almost missed it in the rest of the mail. This is it, I agreed. It was over. I took the missive inside and opened it on the top bunk.

> Well…how's it going mate, the same, or different?

It was fortunate that I appreciated his 'laconic' humour. I thought. And the feeling I could sense, between the lines, that it sought to hide. Many would stop at this point, and throw it away. I read on.

> Here I am writing from my palatial shed, it's

pretty good, very romantic; at least that's what I keep telling myself anyway.

Having been here for a couple of days, just taking it easy. My brain is vaguely back together—at least as much as it could ever be together.

It is twilight; fucking unbelievable countryside at sunset everything is pink—ZAP!

Just like being on drugs!

Was I really with you last week? That place, such alien environments, feels like I'm recovering from undergoing astronomical stress tests, and such sundry stuff.

Have decided to stay put up here—cut myself off from the "world" and try to find a better view of things—I don't work very well with people unfortunately (?) OH WELL, words are very messy—get lost, caught up in them, fucking confused, frustrated etc.

Why am I writing? Good question—I'm just writing that's all, what better things have I got to do? BREATHE yes. I'll concede that one, but why should I breathe (?)—it's getting so as I don't even trust myself these days CRIKEYS—What did Margy say when and if you told her I referenced her as "baggage" HA!

Fucking true though—fucking goddam!

Why did he bother mentioning that? I thought, as I read on.

.... The weird thing about you mate, is, wait for it—I don't think I was ever able to really "relax" with you, in sense of the situation as per we or I—either you had just about managed to clear a space for yourself—or you had travelled away to some goddam fuckin place, and then I would travel, millions of miles to stay just long enough to recover from the journey and be on my way.

Weirdo, don't ya reckon? —Not really?

.... You allowed me to know you, in one sense, but kept "other" parts of yourself fairly separate—that part, probably needed to be protected, exhausted, confused or maybe just biding time—to work out things, this situation—is this annoying you? ... I have to speculate upon these things, hopeless case— tsk, tsk.

...So the gist of this section of the letter is:

It would be too easy to let go—I'm a tenacious son of a bitch—I know you're a suspicious type, allay that if poss.

Would like to know you on friendly terms ...I just like to keep in contact (close physical) with some people—insatiable curiosity—gets me into...

If I can see you again—start from scratch—I will be—enough before I put my foot in it...

It would be superlative to hear from you— just to know what you're up to—

I wasn't overly impressed by his attempts at psychoanalysis. But at the end of the letter were three patches of paint: red, yellow and blue. Next to them the words:

These are the colours for my next canvas— the yellow is a bit off. They are rather magical all the same—I am going to find something rare, something that one can hardly believe exists.

As soon as I had decided it was all over, he sent me a letter. And everything changed.

When a wild pony is being broken-in, the horse moves forward and the horse-breaker backs away, like in a dance. That's the way the breaker gains the horse's trust, they let the horse go to them, let the horse think that's what it wants, so there's no resistance, no fight.

In a way, the power relation is straightforward because the roles are defined by species. Even though the horse has animal power that may temporarily overcome the human, the breaker has power to have the horse there in the first place. Even if a horse throws off a human and the human is killed, other humans have the power to have the horse put to sleep. The equation is simple: humans rule. Humans ride horses not the other way round.

But in a human relationship, how are you supposed to know who is the 'breaker' and who is the 'horse'? When to advance and when to retreat?

Was a horse-breaking analogy even relevant, did a person have to be 'broken' into a relationship and if so did I want to be part of that? Everything remained unclear.

> Couple of hours later—rather large thunder-storm brewing. Had visit from Rex. Said George should be here week after next. I have been working on canvas since then. It is now about 3 pm.
>
> I will definitely be spending the winter in Cairns. Should be good—I envy you the Greek Isles—I wouldn't want to go there just yet— wait for a few years. Next year, after I've been to Adelaide once again will most probably end up

in New Guinea—and various steamy equatorial jungles—I love the humidity—the still intensity—the vibe of places in such weather is spot on—what it does to people, to the landscape, the entire atmosphere, those fans, whirring about, was in café in South Grafton, which is much better than the main town, in café drinking tea, lady fanning herself at extreme end of café, the fan shirring about, had a kink in it, so that every time it went around—clunk, whirr, clunk. Bizarre.

Japan

When I was looking through a box of writing in my old bedroom I found a journal. I opened it and read what I guess I must have written as it was in my handwriting.

<u>Tokyo, Japan, August 6</u>
<u>En route to Australia</u>

At Narita Airport, after claiming my baggage, I was met by two jumping eager Japanese people, a woman and a man, who were anxiously scanning the people in the crowd swirling in all directions in Terminal 1 Arrivals. They were holding up and waving a placard with BERGSON emblazoned upon it in black texta letters. The woman, small dark haired, neat, kept smiling anxiously. I towered above them in my platform leather studded clogs that I bought in Sweden on holiday. They hurried me through the crowds to a waiting car and then we drove down a spaghetti junction of motorways teeming with speeding cars of all descriptions to a skyscraping hotel.

Spent three days in Tokyo and a week in Kyoto, the ancient cultural capital. I don't have a passport stamp for Kyoto but I do have souvenirs of the ryokan, the traditional inn I stayed in with mon pere for six nights, the temples we visited in Kyoto and the shops we went to. I have a phrase book and I've learnt a few words: *kon'nitiha*, hello; *kanpari*, cheers (which they said when we were out with Dad's colleagues and drank sake); and *suki desu ka*, I like it; *kirai desu ka*, I dislike it (useful for new food); *sayonara*, good-bye, with finality.

Before we left Japan we went shopping and bought several printed cotton *yukata*, one for Dad, one for me, and one each for Lily and Margy. They were lightweight cotton kimonos, worn traditionally in bath houses, and now as casual robes, in the house or even outside. There was a great array of designs, in indigo and white on natural foliage themes with a few more colourful ones.

"They'll be ideal Christmas presents. Lily can have hers at Christmas in Australia, and I'll send Margy hers, in Northern Ireland," I said deliberating over yukata patterns. I considered buying a decorative obi sash to go with my yukata but I settled for the casual tie that came with it made of the same fabric.

"What about one for Mum?" I said suddenly realising she had been forgotten.

"Do you think she'd like one?" said Dad.

"I don't know."

"I don't really think she would," he said.

So we didn't buy a yukata for Mum.

That was to turn out to be a mistake, that I still regret.

Canberra, November 15, 1976

Looking forward to the others arriving. Mum, Lily, Alex, Sarah. It's been difficult being here for these four months. I don't know a single person my own age in the whole southern hemisphere... That is a sobering thought. I wish I could have stayed, with my friends, and helped pack up and sell The Old Parsonage. Maybe I was lucky leaving early. Missing school... The sixth form college I am going to go to is still being built, and I'm having yet more time off school.

They're due to arrive on Christmas Eve. Best Xmas present ever.

<u>December 24</u>

Going to pick them up at the airport! It is very hot now. Fantastic seeing them all again!

. . . — — . . . . . . — — . . .

. . . — — . . . . . . — — . . .

. . . — — . . . . . . — — . . .

We drove back to the house the family has been allocated by the government; it's just temporary till we find a house, Dad keeps on having to say to Mum and Lily. A bungalow. On the outskirts of a half-built suburb! On first sight, immediate—unvarnished—reaction of horror—from Mum and Lily! They hate it. Even despite all the work Dad and I have done to it to make the best of it. Dad sanded and polished the floorboards in the living room, and hallway and bedrooms. He made a Japanese garden in the back yard, in an enclosure fenced off with wire. I sanded and polished turn-of-the-century dressing tables with mirrors that we bought in a shop that Dad and I rode to on new bicycles. I sanded and polished one for me and one for Lily.

Mum and Lily very upset and angry. They feel no need to hide or temper down their disbelief, and aversion.

We're crammed into a matchbox!

<u>Xmas Day</u>

The day is hot and strained like toxic tea. Mum and siblings are struck down by jet lag and heat. There was an extended outpouring of disbelief, disgust and fury, and heat, from Lily.
Probably the best that can be said is—it is very, very hot.

Mum is not overjoyed. She is exhausted, after all the hard work of packing up and selling the house. Dad has been constructing built-in wardrobes in the bedrooms but they're not quite finished, and the doors don't work properly.
Everything is topsy-turvy. Upside Down. Surreal unreality.
Unwrapping presents. Lily unwrapped her yukata. I chose it after much deliberation for her, it has a grey and red-pink flowering tree pattern on white background, in contrast to the traditional indigo with white bamboo patterns that I selected for myself and Margarita, and that Dad also chose.
"A kimono!" she said, laughing. "Thanks!"
"It's a yukata, they're much lighter weight." I said. "Kimonos are made of silk. These are much more casual, made of cotton; you can wear it as a bathrobe, or a summer dressing gown. We got one for Margy, too, I sent it to her for Christmas."
"Didn't *everyone* get a kimono?" asked Mum.
Dad didn't reply. He was looking thoughtfully at a book on topiary.
Lily was putting it on over her dress, she stood up. "Where's a mirror I want to see what it looks like!"
"We didn't think anyone else would like one," I said.
"I would have thought kimonos would have been an ideal

gift for *everyone...*" Mum said.

I looked down and opened another present.

"A scarab-beetle back scratcher! Thanks Alex!"

In the bedroom we were now sharing, Lily saw me getting changed for dinner and started to cry.

"You're so thin," she sobbed. "What's happened to you?"

Outside the sun burnt a hole in the sky.

Sayonara, Baby

The train pulled into Grafton station. Night was falling. I shouldered my backpack. Stepped off, and stopped. I stood on the platform looking around. A few people had disembarked from the train, a woman and baby met by an elderly man, hurrying away; a tall, fit-looking man—flannelette checked shirt, jeans—with a neat beard, was talking with the stationmaster, a corpulent man with a long beard, in uniform; his loud confident voice boomed through the thickening dusk.

I extracted the folded piece of paper with Ray's cousin's address from my backpack pocket and unfolded it; well…I guessed I would have to set off to… wherever it was. I walked out of Grafton station and stopped again.

An empty car park sloped upwards to a road. Beyond the road was a ragged fringe of dark tall trees, wooden houses on high stilt legs, was this sub-tropical outer suburbia?

No shops in sight. Not a person to be seen.

The sky was darkening, clouds were purple-black, air hot and close with humidity. I turned back towards the lights of the station.

The bearded man who'd been talking to the stationmaster

was walking purposefully towards the only vehicle in the car park, a white four-wheel drive.

Clutching my piece of paper, I strode quickly towards him.

"Excuse me. Do you know how to get to—" I glanced at the paper, "Styx Creek Crossing?" I smiled with a full-wattage of determined charm. He paused, his hand on the car door.

"Styx Creek Crossing?" he repeated slowly.

"Yes," I said. "I'm trying to get to a friend's place. I don't s'pose you know where I could get a bus?" He looked doubtful.

"You won't get a bus out there. Buses don't go out there. It's right out in the forest."

"In the forest?" I tried not to think of Little Red Riding Hood.

"You're trying to get to your friend's place?" He was looking at me appraisingly.

"Yeah, that's right. I've never been there before. I've just come up from Sydney. It's forty k's from Grafton."

His face tightened in sudden resolution.

"Well, I'll take you out there, if you want. I'm driving out in that direction. Some of the way, anyhow." He unlocked the vehicle. As I thanked him, I stepped up, pulling myself up into the front seat.

Taking a lift from a stranger was risky. But I was used to the risk. I began hitching in Northern Ireland, when I had to get home after the last bus had stopped, in the term when I was kept in detention almost every day after school, for things like forgetting to bring the right textbook. I was only thirteen. Nothing happened to me. I had a good instinct for who's okay and who's not, I told myself, I was on edge, fully focused, and determined. But this was all part of the adventure. There was no other way I could have got out there.

"I'm Georgiou," he said as we left the town behind.

"Roxy," I replied firmly, turning to look at him. "Pleased to meet you." Georgiou wanted to know the details of my journey. Where had I come from? Who was I going to see?

He wanted to talk. I was used to the hitchhikers' bargain. In return for your lift, I couldn't think 'your life', you answer questions, talk willingly, with polite enthusiasm, you laugh at the driver's jokes, humour them, on your best behaviour, but with a hard veneer of assertiveness, a willed psychic strength, which is your protection, so even a serial killer couldn't think thoughts about you. And all of this is a risky inner thrill.

It was quite a bit further from Grafton than I'd imagined it would be. A few miles out of town, when we were still on the sealed road, we passed an intersection. "That's my turn-off," Georgiou said. "But I'll drive you a bit further out, though," he added. I hope so, I thought.

We hit the unsealed road, the dirt track. The road wound deeper into the rainforest. After we'd been driving for about an hour, Georgiou was getting upset. Several rocks had flown up from the track hitting the underside of his vehicle.

"My petrol tank could get punctured," he said. "We should have reached it by now..." He sounded alarmed.

"Well, it says here it's just after Styx Creek, there should be a gate off a turning, on the left side of the road," I said, helpfully, squinting at the directions Ray had sent. Georgiou was clearly a decent kind of guy. Not the kind to abandon a young traveller in the middle of a forest, in the middle of the night. At least that's what I hoped. His annoyed noises were growing louder; rocks kept flying under the tires, hitting the vehicle's undercarriage. I felt anxious. What if his directions were wrong? What if I didn't find it? What then? The driver drove across a ford over a creek, to the left of which I could see a five-barred farm gate.

"That's it!" I called. Georgiou put on the brakes.

Through the bars of the gate, the four-wheel drive's headlights picked out a field, a dirt track, but there were no lights. No house to be seen.

"That was really great. Thanks. I don't know what I would have done—" I started to open the door.

"I'll take you there," said Georgiou. He sounded excited.

"It's okay, I'm sure I can find it from here."

I was suddenly starting to feel excited about surprising Ray.

"No, no, I'll take you there," the driver insisted.

I jumped down from the four-wheel drive, and opened the gate, which he drove through. I closed it, behind the vehicle, and climbed back in. We drove down a steep dip in the field, and up again like a roller-coaster, over a hilltop, and then saw the lights in the pitch blackness ahead, I remembered that Ray had said his cousin and his wife were living in a barn they'd built. One day they would build a house.

A patch of light appeared in the darkness, a long haired bearded figure ran out of a doorway, shrieking and screaming and waving a shotgun at us.

"What the fuck do you fuckers want? Stop right there!! Fuck off you bastards, go on fuck off or I'll kill ya!!! I'll fuckin kill ya!!!" He pointed the gun at the four-wheel drive.

"Christ," said Georgiou beside me. I heard his sharp intake of breath. I stared through the windscreen with interest. Ray had said that his cousin was wild.

"It's okay," I said. "That must be Rex, my friend's cousin."

"Your friend's cousin—who is your friend anyway?"

I opened the car door and climbed out, calling loudly.

"Hello! Rex! Rex? Rex? I'm Roxy— a friend of Ray's—is Ray here?"

"What?" The wild man waved his gun; he was staring at me. "Roxy? You're Roxy? You're looking for Ray?"

"Yes," I said, walking towards him. "I'm sorry I didn't get in touch before. I know it's a bit unexpected. Is Ray here?"

"Netta, Netta!" Rex called back through the door of the barn. "Roxy's here! It's Roxy!" (I was surprised that he seemed to know about me.) "Roxy's here! Come in! Come in!" He said. "Ray's at the lean-to, the shack, that's where he's staying, down the track. We'll go down there in a few minutes..."

It was only when we were all standing in the barn that he asked, "And who's this?" looking at my companion with open hostility.

"Georgiou," he said, smiling and stepping forward with his hand outstretched.

"Fuck off," said Rex, stepping back with a sneer.

Georgiou stayed. To my surprise. He shared the joint of homegrown, rolled by Rex, I declined, and he even accompanied us as we set off to find Ray. We all walked down the hill, me and Rex and Netta with Georgiou, through dark trees, oil-lantern swinging in Rex's hand as we traversed leaf-covered ground, over a rise, and there appeared a light ahead, glowing in the darkness. We stepped across a ford of stones in a shallow creek, and then I saw a vision, stumbling out from a shack, in blue shorts, with bare torso, looking puzzled and sleepy.

"What are you doing here?" Ray looked like he could not believe his eyes. As if I were a kind of apparition.

"I just happened to be in the area and I thought I'd drop

in for a visit," I said, airily, managing to keep a straight face.

Later he said that he'd believed me, he really thought that I was with Georgiou, driving along through rainforest outside Grafton, in the middle of the night, in the middle of nowhere, and decided to call in on him. He said he thought Georgiou was my new boyfriend.

And nothing I could say or do could change his mind.

Early morning. Not sure of day or date. Decided to go down to river for swim. Nearby a half-built house on stilts, perched in tall sub-tropical trees above the river. Ray said it belongs to an architect who comes down every few months. There's a rainwater tank outside the house, we fill water bottles there—closer than Rex and Netta's barn.

Very sensual swim—feeling like the missing link between Lady Godiva, Ophelia and Lady of Shalott—pure sensation, drifting, eyes shut, on the surface of the water, green air, gold light, mermaid girl.

On either side the river Clarence lie…deep forests that hide the sky… Slither up onto riverbank, dripping, into sunlight. Walk along track past the architect's house, on my way back to shack. Delicious feeling, walking through shady fragrant forest, only the cotton of my yukata between warm moist air and skin. I spy Ray at the tap, filling a water bottle. He looks up at me blankly. We haven't slept together the last couple of nights, but instead have both lain snugly zipped up in our sleeping bags, on opposite sides of the small shack—which has one side open to the rainforest. Developing the concept of single sleeping bag as full-body chastity belt.

Ray was living off intoxicants, over-proof rum, homegrown dope, and the occasional "magic mushroom" that he found in the forest. As he worked, every now and then, he wandered out from his studio to consult one of the few books he brought with him, which he kept on the car seat next to the fireplace. *Food of the Deities*, a hardcover tome, detailing a history and geography of humanity's divinely inspired relationship with intoxicants, with full colour illustrations.

He was obsessed with his work, absorbed in his drawings. He rarely left his studio, I heard him sometimes muttering to himself. "Trying to find something rare, no-one will believe it can exist…" I'd been sketching and reading quietly. I hadn't felt like drinking over-proof rum. I wanted to connect with the landscape, my feelings, in the atmosphere of the forest, with nothing to intercept the direct sensations of my experience.

He'd been faintly contemptuous, which had irritated me and made me withdraw from him. But I was happy to see him at the tap.

"Hi," I said.

"Yep," he replied. "Do you want to go into the house?"

I followed him up the steep ladder into the large half-built space, which had a completed floor, the frames of walls, and windows, overlooking the river. The air felt close, warm on my skin. Golden rays filtered through the canopy of ferns. The sounds of birds, fragrance of forest vegetation, rich sensual morning light, and nature-rush; what could be more natural than being here in the rainforest? All the whispering magic of the trees around us…

He lay on the floor on his back on the wooden floorboards. I lay on top of him, cushioned by his body. His body hardened. Froze beneath me. He turned his head away. I sat up, and so did he. "What's wrong?" I asked. "Don't you feel like making love, *darling?*"

"No, I don't. And I'm not going to."

"What?"

He was putting on his tee-shirt. His face was pale and expression deadly serious.

"You don't mean it?"

"Yes I do. It's not right."

"What are you talking about: not right?"

"I'm waiting for the right woman." Now he was pulling on his shorts.

I looked at him in disbelief. He could not mean this. What about his letters?? And then it clicked: Georgiou, or whatever he was called. "God, you don't still think I was really going out with that guy do you? How many times do I have to tell you…?"

But he was bending down and picking up the water bottle.

"I'm going back to the hut."

I watched him disappear down the stairwell as if descending through a stage trapdoor that swallowed up his feet first, then his legs, torso, shoulders. His head, last to go, topped by wicked flame red locks.

Sayonara, baby.

I sat in the unfinished room, amidst skeletal bones of hope. The architect would be happy, one day he or she would have a house. Waves of bird song, river music, advanced, receded. I looked around, at raw joists, naked frames, plasterboards piled in a stack. Out here in paradise, walls were going up everywhere.

I stood up, brushing sawdust off my skin, and gingerly

climbed down the ladder; he'd had enough time to get back, I didn't want him to think I could be following him. I walked slowly back along the narrow forest track, trying hard not to feel like Little Riding Hood.

There was not much to pack: a change of clothes, a couple of books, *Rimbaud*; Borge's *Gold of the Tigers*.

When it was done, I sat on log on the packed earthen floor of the lean-to, and opened the poetry book at random. I read about people leaving, forgetting that their flesh is burning and flayed from where Christ's priest laid his hands. And the Priest is meanwhile provided with the sheltering shade of the roof of a leafy arbour.

I would leave, with sunburn, Raymond working beneath the shade roof of his shack, and I would go once more out into the sun, to travel across the land, by 'rule of thumb', shouldering my backpack of dreams, hitching my luck to the endless afternoon, and just hope I'll get a lift.

I put Rimbaud in my backpack, with my diary, the decaffeinated coffee and the water bottle that I'd filled at the architect's house. I'd eaten all the apples I'd brought with me.

Ray was working in his studio at the back of the shack.

I walked to the doorway and looked in at him, bent over one of the elaborately detailed sketches he'd been immersed in since before my arrival. Ray Furnett, a long-distance swimmer of Art, scarcely able to raise his head above the creative briny to accept food from a support boat. Working on studies for paintings, whose optical illusions would supposedly stagger and confound, open a crack in the material world of illusion to reveal the truth of infinity beyond…

He'd outlined his methodology: using mathematics to try to find elusive intangible things, to transport the artist and viewer into undiscovered states of perception. I had accepted this. Beware, stand back, genius at work... Attempting orbit of the sun... Prepare for blast-off, etcetera.

Now, I wondered, what was he really doing? I didn't see any evidence of his heroic metaphysical quest. All there seemed to be to show for it were a few geometric drawings, and bits of rubbish he'd found. A couple of coke cans and crisps packets, faded sweets wrappers that he'd nailed on the makeshift walls. An 'ironic' counterpart to the collages of leaves he had made in his parent's garage in suburban Adelaide that I'd been so taken by, all those millions of years ago.

We speak at the same time.

"George is arriving tomorrow," said Ray, not looking up.

"I'm going to go." I said.

I stood in the doorway, staring at his back. His familiar naked torso, pink-white skin, blue shorts, gold hair lit up by the light stealing through the windows, cracks in the walls…

"I said, I'm GOING TO GO."

"Wha—" he spun around, looking dazed and bemused.

"Go? Where?"

"Canberra." I gazed through the windows, past his head.

"I don't care if George is coming tomorrow. Whoever he is. You haven't even bothered to tell me about him anyway."

Lime-green grass irradiated in the dazzling morning light, glowing as if lit from within. Who but a dullard would need drugs out here? I shifted my line of vision and turned upon my ex what I meant to be a controlled hard glare.

"When?"

"Today. Now. No time like the present, the train leaves at six this evening. I'll walk through the forest and hitch a lift to Grafton on the main road. It could take a few hours."

He was looking at me as if he didn't believe it.

I stood in the doorway prolonging the satisfaction of seeing his shock. Perhaps it was something of a double standard after all my former prevarications, but what did he think I'd do, if not leave? He said he was waiting for the right woman. Well, let him wait.

He walked me to the sealed road to Grafton, seven k's down the winding road, through the forest. We hardly spoke. The air seemed thinner, less substantial, against my striding body. As if it had lost some of its heavy hypnotic humidity, its hold over me. I was glad of the chance to stretch my legs, to really walk somewhere. The beaten track became sealed road before it reached the highway. We stopped as we reached the tarmac.

"Well, I'll leave you here, skipper," Ray said. "Hope you get a lift alright."

"I will," I said. "Bye."

He turned and we walked away from each other.

"Say hello to George from me." I shouted behind me sarcastically as an after-thought.

And that was that.

I walked on by myself. I was walking away from Ray, and the day felt flat. Dull and flat, empty. A moment of Nothingness expands to soul-consuming proportions...

It's not so bad I tried to tell myself. You've only lost the love of your life: "Light of days and nights".

Ha! I had to keep on going. I gazed resolutely across the paddocks I was passing through, in a clearing in the forest. I remembered riding along this same road with Sam a couple of years ago. Samuel was in Israel on a kibbutz, connecting with his Jewish roots, "Trying to get over our break-up."

He'd been sending me newsy, detailed letters, recounting the minutiae of his life there. He was picking oranges in orchards, sharing a dormitory at night, waking at dawn to see the watchman performing 'his ablutions' in Samuel's words, over a bucket. Communal meals, olive groves, body building exercise: Samuel's structured, ordered world, transported from Australia to Israel. It seemed like forever since we'd split up.

I reached the main road and stopped. I didn't have a watch. After a long time, a white car appeared around the corner. I stuck out my thumb, smiling, willing it to stop. It sped by obliviously.

An undefined period of time expanded as I sat on the grass at the side of the road.

The steady rumble of an engine approached from the west.

A largish truck appeared around the bend in the road. I jumped up and stuck out my thumb. The truck swerved to a halt and I ran to meet it.

"Hi," I called looking up. There were two young blonde guys, the driver and one in the passenger seat who opened the door and called down, "Where ya goin'?"

"I'm going to Grafton."

"You can have a ride in the back if you want, there's no room in here."

"Okay, thanks,' I said, picking up my backpack.

"Sure ya wanna to go in there?" He asked with a big smile.

I glanced around at the back of the small truck.

"Yes," I replied. Why wouldn't I?

He jumped onto the road and I followed him to the back of the truck. It was a small container, like a removal van. The back opened. He unlocked it and swung open the sealed door. The interior was empty and it looked pretty dark in there.

"You sure you'll be alright in there?" he asked again, looking at me quizzically.

I gazed into the confined space. It wasn't going to be comfortable, but it was only forty k's I calculated, and I had to get there soon or I'd miss the train, and that just couldn't happen.

"If you're not okay, give us a yell and we'll stop," he said as I scrambled up into the container, about one and a half meters off the ground.

"Okay," I said, brightly.

He closed the door. It slammed shut with a great clang that shook the whole truck.

As soon it was closed, I found out what was carried in the truck. Fish. The stench was overpowering.

The truck drove off. I could feel every bump in the road, amplified. It felt as if there were continuous bumps and craters, which rattled the truck, and shook and jarred my body. It was pitch dark, stiflingly claustrophobic, and the smell was nauseating. It wasn't long before my head began spinning with vertigo, I felt dizzy and faint; I was panting as if I had been running for miles, gasping for air. I realized that the truck was a sealed container, and the oxygen was running out. I crawled to the driver's end and banged on the metal wall, shouting to the maximum extent my lungs could reach:

"Hello! Hello! Stop the truck!!" Nothing happened. After shouting until my lungs hurt, I realized it was pointless. They wouldn't be able to hear me in the front above the thundering roar of the engine.

They must have known that, just as they must have known there was no air in here.

I feebly crawled back to the door.

I would die in here, when the oxygen ran out. How long

would that be? Judging by how I felt now it could be fifteen minutes, at the most... I was almost passing out. So, this was it, this was how my life would end... in the back of a stinking truck. It couldn't. I was determined not to die.

That's when I saw a glimmer of light in the darkness; the size of a pinprick on the lowest side of the door that I would be thanking Goddess for, and recounting in stories for years to come. I crawled close, and stared at the light, a minute hole in the thick rubber seal. It was old, cracked, worn and torn, and a speck of brilliant piercing light was shining through. Where there was light there was air. Digging my fingernails into the rubber seal, I poked and tore at the tiny crack, making it larger. I put my mouth against it, and breathed in deeply; I remained there for the rest of the journey. Crouched in stifling, rattling darkness, in the airless stench of dead fish, sucking air through the rubber, thanking Goddess for small mercies, minute cracks and gaps, my chance to keep on breathing.

Eventually the truck ground and shuddered to a halt. The door was pulled open. I reeled with the impact of light, fresh air, the world. Life! I was still alive. The blonde guy standing before me was watching me very closely I thought suspiciously, laughing as if at some big private joke—had he really tried to kill me?

"Okay?" he asked, peering at me darkly.

"Yes." I slid out of the truck and staggered onto terra firma, holding my backpack.

"Thanks for the lift."

Calling his bluff. I was determined not to give him what would possibly be the satisfaction of knowing what I'd been through in the back of his truck. I'd got here, that was all that mattered.

The truck had stopped above the railway station, next to the car park. At almost exactly the same spot I'd set off from, in Georgiou's four-wheel drive, to go to find Ray six days ago.

As I walked down the hill to the station, every step I took felt like bouncing on a trampoline. The stench of fish remained in my nostrils for a long time after I was comfortably ensconced on the southbound train, sipping State Railways wine, trying to forget everything that had just happened. My Grafton trip, my dream lover. My cynicism deepened and took hold.

Music

Margarita was cold on my return. She would hardly say a word, let alone look at me. It was only when I assured her, and reassured her, that we had split up, it had been a disaster, we hadn't got on, that she began to relent a little.

"I find him physically repulsive," I said as we sat out on Isobel's terrace. An image of his turned back flashed into my thoughts. "He has soft arms."

She gave me an odd look—Hello? But I could see she was beginning to relax a little. "I find him physically repulsive," I repeated.

"I'm thinking about taking classical violin again," she said. "I played in Ballyhope Youth Orchestra until I was almost thirteen. That is, until just before I met you."

There was an unmistakable edge of accusation in her voice. Surely she was not implying there was a connection between that and my arrival at Grammar School.

"You weren't playing in the orchestra when I arrived," I said. "Do you think the imminence of my arrival into your life was so momentous that it could it have caused Time to go backwards?"

"Daddy taught me from when I was three."

I looked at her long musician's fingers draped elegantly around the stem of Mum's bohemian crystal goblet.

"What about your electric violin?" I said. "What's wrong with that? It's brilliant, you have to stick with it!'

Margarita composed new electric violin music. I thought it was inspired music. And it epitomized an ethos by which I thought we both were living: expressing ourselves, letting go, and living in the moment NOW! I'd watched her on stage in the spotlight in her black dress, playing electric violin with the band. I'd danced to her violin, in streets and in nightclubs. Margarita playing classical violin, I couldn't see it. Didn't want to see it...

She took little bird-sips of her drink, running her hand meditatively through the jet of water arcing from the lion's open jaws. Sighing seriously and sadly to herself, as if she knew things that were way beyond my understanding.

But I, at least, knew what I was doing. I was going to return to Adelaide to begin Second Year. And I had no one to go with, since I'd left Samuel, my ex-ex-boyfriend for Raymond last year. Then left Raymond—who was now, it seemed, my ex-boyfriend—a week ago.

Now as she spent hours practicing piano and violin, I felt there was not so much a wall between us as a thin veil, which I could easily push aside if I wanted to. Later.

A few nights later I asked her to move to Adelaide with me.

"Well, alright," she said in a serious tone. "But you'd better not change your mind."

"Of course I won't. There's no way I'm ever having anything to do with him again."

...Have been attempting a bit of writing—the energy is amazing—falling into language like a mirror—a labyrinth—winding and unwinding— as our dear friend would say! Which one is he anyway?

How are Margy, and other sundry satellite personalities, the same? I hope not!

I miss ya sport...

I must like you in some way—I never or hardly ever forsake any of the paper out of me notebook——let alone for letters—a precedent has been set!—I never could abide by the bounds of habit.

Lily was very middle class—wasn't she! By golly—oh well—we aren't are we?

The next morning his third letter arrived. On my return from the shops to buy milk, I saw a familiar long white missive protruding from the mailbox. My nerve endings shrieked like subliminal fruit bats at the sight of it. A long white envelope with bulging sides—I carefully extracted Ray's letter from the rest of the mail—my name and Isobel's address inscribed in blue biro, the sloping whorls of his handwriting. Suddenly the morning was significant, every action resonating with heightened meaning.

I walked inside, forgot about making coffee. From Alex's room I could hear the steady tinkle of scales being repeated over. If I went onto the front porch, Margarita might come out for breakfast whilst I was reading the letter and see it. I didn't want her to know that Ray had written to me, again. I closed the bedroom door behind me, climbed the ladder and

sat on the bunk. Slitting open the envelope, I pulled out the
wad of folded pages. Smoothing the papers with both hands,
I leaned back on pillows propped against the wall, and began
to read:

        Well this is   the endso don't read this
                        some poet bloke
thought
of it before   novelty, I hate novelty
       full-on-honesty
which can be INTIMIDATING
                You confuse me
                But I love it
      See ya
         BEGIN HERE
            ...

...   ...
  goodness,
howdoesone begin a
    letter to, well,
whoever you are!
    . . .

     you confuse me   but I
  love
it   BEGIN HERE
    . . .
      .
  .   ...

  you
    confuse
   me

but

                         I

           LOVE
              it
you confuseme
    but

                      I love it

I confused him…that was charming, after how he'd treated me…but he loved it. Could he have discovered I was 'the right woman', after I left?

My dear one—
    Sitting in "that" café in main Grafton, the one with the tired waitresses, the awesome burden of life, those poor wretches...HAH!
    Received a group valentine from the Art Scandals back in Adelaide— imaginative letter. HA HA — at least some think of me with love (sigh).
    What are you up to now—bet you screwed your way all the way back to Canberra. All those penises like daggers in my heart...

I had no idea where Ray's ideas about my supposed infidelity were coming from. And he thought that I was suspicious...

If you could have only stayed—the moon—the evenings here are wonderful—voluminous skies, insect life on the planet moron. Yesterday whilst on my daily constitutional (minor peruse about the estate of my antediluvian landscape) lo! Behold! There, right before me glasses! Pert on a cow-pat! NYAH!

½ dozen magic ones whoo—ZIP

reality shift—where was I anyway, not here, not there, tomorrow on the full moon.
9.00 pm synchronize your watches boys its cup of magic teatime!

I hope I will survive! (HAH!) Ahhh! sup slurp sup slurp! My I'm a pig—wallow oink! dry humour to boot...

I really do feel the urge to leave. It is becoming too comfortable—still haven't completed "the painting." "Boy Ray wrestling the angel of light" tee hee!

...I hope you are in superlative excellence, my dearest one! May everything come your way! I am looking forward to our next confused meeting! I have rediscovered that I enjoy your presence dangerously—if only it were even more so!

...the Cocteau! ah yes opened at terrible heroes, HOLY TERRORS.

....

....

(goes on)
Yours orgasm seeking organism   DOE

Despite everything, including the fact he'd written in the persona of his alter ego, I found myself wanting to see Ray again, wanting to be with him. I read his letter several times, in bed. He said he planned to return to Canberra in a week's time. Margarita and I had decided to visit the Farm for a few days, before leaving for Adelaide. He did not mention George. Maybe he had not arrived after all. Maybe George was just a figment of his deranged imagination.

That night, Margy and I relaxed on the front porch in the warm air. She had vodka and tonic; I was drinking white wine from a cask in the fridge.

"I think Raymond is thinking of going to the Farm at some point, before the end of summer," I observed casually.

"Really," she said, acidly. "Well I hope it's not when we're there. Although it would be just typical if that's when he does turn up."

Margy and Ray appeared to have developed a mutual long distance hostility towards each other.

"No, I don't think we need to worry about that, he has to prepare his show in Adelaide, it wouldn't be until much later."

Margy and I caught the train to Cooma.

We walked down the main street from the railway station, stopping as usual at the café, for a cappuccino.

We sat down on a bench seat at the far end. The back wall was covered in flags of all the nations of workers on the Snowy Scheme. There were newspapers on the table, and a plaque on the wall next to the table. As we waited for the coffees I read the wall plaque, which told the story of the Snowy Mountains Hydro-Electric Scheme, and the pioneering role the founder of the Neapolitan played in bringing café culture, and real coffee, to the workers on the Snowy Scheme in the mountains.

SNOWY HYDRO-ELECTRIC SCHEME, BIRTHPLACE OF AUSTRALIAN MULTI-CULTURALISM

The Snowy Scheme is the greatest feat of engineering ever seen in Australia. Harnessing the power of the Snowy River, to syphon to the Murray-Darling basin for agriculture, and creating clean electric power for six states. It is also a great social achievement of a scale never before seen in Australia, if not the world. Founded in 1949, it saw the massive influx and assisted immigration of over 100,000 workers from postwar Europe. Workers from over thirty countries carried out the construction work of the Snowy Scheme, with most hailing from Europe. Many migrants were fleeing the devastation left by the war, and were given the chance to start a new life in Australia. Many who had been enemies worked side by side in the harsh conditions of the Snowy Scheme, blasting transmission lines through the mountains. Along with their brawn they brought their culture, and new cuisines came to the high country.

I suddenly remembered what the guy in red leather trousers had said at the party that had been so disturbing.

"That's funny," I turned to Margarita who was also reading it. "About all the people who came here and worked in the mountains. You know I met a guy in a party in Adelaide, a friend of Ray's I think. Diana had told us about a man who moved in next to their studio in Sydney, who was saying all kinds of horrible, horrific things to the artists, about what he did in the war in Croatia, brutally murdering children."

"WHAT?" said Margy.

"Yes. The guy told her to be careful and started telling us these stories about how writers are being spied on by people who were fascists and war criminals who were allowed to leave Germany and Croatia and Italy and come here. They make a living from it he said, in some agency, to do with the cold war. But I think he said that they were recruited to work on the Snowy Mountains Scheme, which is how they were allowed to come here."

"*What?*" said Margy again. "Really?"

"That's what he said and he seemed to know what he was talking about, he said he was almost murdered himself. That's the other thing he said. That these monsters, really evil people who killed children came here, and they are still doing it, he said they are the ones who are behind the murders that have been happening, of hitchhikers, that have been in the news. The terrible things in Adelaide, the abductions, and murders of teenage boys."

"I haven't been following the news."

"Neither have I. It's too horrific." I said.

I flipped over the newspaper on the table in front of me.

"As I was saying."

We gazed at the front-page headline:

MUTILATED BODY OF YOUTH FOUND IN BIN BAG ON ADELAIDE RIVERBANK

Police are treating the mutilated body as possibly related to the spate of abductions and murders in Adelaide, including the hitchhiker murders.

"Oh my God," said Margarita.

"How terrible. Thank God nothing happened to me when I hitched into the forest to see Ray."

"You *hitched* there?"

"Yes. It was forty kilometres out in the forest, I couldn't get there any other way. There were no buses out there."

"For goodness sake, Roxy, you're mad."

"Well I didn't know it was like that. I'm not doing it again. He didn't even appreciate my effort."

"I hope we'll be okay at the Farm. It's totally isolated."

"Of course we will be. That's why it's so safe."

"Well we're not hitching there."

"I thought we were going to walk?"

"We are. And we'd better get going right now." She said in her Miss Manners tone.

"It's only twelve kilometres, shouldn't take more than three hours. We'll be there in time for tea!"

We picked up our backpacks, and set off, on the pavement heading south down main street. Reaching the end of town we walked on the side of the road, the hard tarmac, single-file, to the Old Western Plain Road, then turned right off the road and immediately my spirits lifted, we were well on our way.

We walked past fields of cars, the colourful car graveyards; past the golf course, the first large homestead farm, and on to the unsealed road. We walked in companionable silence down the dirt road as the high country of the Monaro Plain spread out like an invitation. Scrubby fields split with ochre cracks of erosion gullies, green-lichened grey rocks. At the edge of the paddocks, white hands of ghost gums pointed fingers towards the sky. Wallabies and kangaroos abounded. Far away down the valley the distant peaks of the Mountains shimmered and hovered, drawing us onwards.

The road twisted around sheer sides of small mountains. We kept walking as the shadows lengthened, and the countryside turned purple; the evening aroma of cooling earth arose like a deep soul food. This was the first time I had been here alone with Margy. Every other time I'd been here in a twosome had been with Samuel, on his motorbike. He'd progressed from the vintage 500 cc, to the flashy Italian 750 cc with chrome petrol tank, to the 1000 cc we travelled Australia on. So many times had I ridden this road with Samuel that the curves were ingrained into my sensory memory; the precipitous drop to the red dried-out creek bed, the adrenalin of the rough road with no crash-barriers to misjudgement. Margy was walking slightly behind me, breathing audibly beneath the weight of her backpack; in front of me shadows lengthened, darkening stripes across the white stones and dust of the dirt track.

We kept on walking down the valley, fording the first creek, up the hill then down and over the second, splashing through shallow water, balancing on stepping stones, then up and over the next hillside, climbing the second last hill, we were on the home stretch, almost there... we crested the last hill, catching a glimpse of the farmhouse in the shelter of our mountain.

"Creek's low," I said.

Our section of creek stretched before us, bounding the Farm to east and south, west was bounded by the lower slopes of the mountain and north by the Murrumbidgee river. We walked down the hill to the splashing border stream intersecting the track, the third ford; it was precarious, balancing on slippery stones mostly submerged underwater. We walked onwards, to the gate; off the road, pushed it open into our property, walking up the track towards the house, through the home-paddock and the compound that all our family under Dad's direction spent a year clearing stones from. The house was as it always was. It was there. Waiting for us for when we arrived.

Margarita was staying in her room off the kitchen. I was, as always, in my room, a large airy space separate to the rest of the house that opened off the far side of the front veranda.

It felt different with Margarita to how it always had been with Samuel who, as my de facto husband, had stayed in my room without anything needing to be said or negotiated.

Now that Margarita was here I felt that I needed my own space.

Suddenly everything seemed somehow messy, unresolved between us, raw and ragged. I sat on Grandmother's old pink floral armchair on the veranda and gazed in front of me to the creek, the cleared hillside beyond. Everything here in the landscape looked to be waiting... Waiting for some sign above to give it meaning.

Yet, the signs I had to bestow, my invocations of ancient Greek landscapes, never quite connected with the shimmering land that eluded my gaze. I always felt that I did not belong here. It was too hot or too cold, or too vast …No matter how much I tried to be at home I felt like an alien.

On an afternoon that was too hot for walks, we took photos. I saw Margarita walking around the side of the old wooden farmhouse in her black silk slip, wearing, as a sun hat, a home-made beekeeper hat encircled with a green muslin veil. From the apple trees, I started snapping. When she saw me she burst out laughing, and held her slip out at each side, like an Irish dancer. The next photos I took in close-up. Margarita peering ironically from under the veil that she had thrown back over the beekeeper hat. Her long dark eyelashes framed her eyes, she mock-pouted 'seductively' in a 'Mata Hari' moue.

I brought her image into focus, as she broke into a high kicking dance routine, spun with arms held above her head, and burled around the side of the wooden house.

The next series of photos I took were of Margarita in the farmhouse kitchen, playing violin in her black silk slip. It was easier to focus inside, where the light was not so bright.

Margarita had invited a friend of ours, Raphael Granville,

a fellow musician to stay. He arrived in his car with his oboe. The small mountain echoed for hours on end to the sounds of their playing.

I had felt uncomfortable in Raff's presence, ever since my sister Lily had told me what he had supposedly told her, about what Raff had found under the bed of his father who had a high position in the church. What those terrible things had shown about men in frocks, men of the cloth, in frocks, men of the church, more like *Our Lady of the Flowers* by Jean Genet, than Our Father. Yes, shocking things, about abuse of minors, boys, she said, he said he had found, that I did not want to know, under the Bishop's bed. I couldn't tell anyone, I was worried about my mother. She was a parishioner at Raff's father's cathedral, a devout follower of the faith. I knew she would not believe me, or my sister, and she might be angry towards me if I said such a terrible thing about the Bishop. I tried to forget it. I had to act as if I did not know when I saw Raff, as my sister was not supposed to tell anyone. We just had to act as if everything was normal. Maybe Raff was wrong, or making it up. Maybe it had not happened. But why would he have said such a thing? It was not the kind of thing the son of a bishop would say without an actual cause. It was not the kind of thing someone could make a mistake about. Raff was a lovely highly intelligent person. No one could do anything, and we all had to pretend it had not happened, or was not happening. Margarita's friend in the band she played electric violin with in Melbourne, whose father was a scoutmaster, had said a similar thing to her about his father. How his father had abused the scouts. The songs he wrote and sang were manic, postmodern, pastiche kitsch. Art was the way to escape and comment on the sickness of society, and the establishment.

It added to the discomfort building up in the house like the heat, which was unbearable.

Outside the air shimmered, cicadas screamed, the sun burned through days that passed in a white heat, white light haze.

And then he arrived.

I was sitting on the front porch in the middle of the day gazing into the hazy, pale green creek willows, when above the trees, I spotted a small, determined figure. Rounding the bend in the unsealed road, which curved out of sight behind a low grey-green hill.

Who was that?

My nerves shrieked.

It couldn't be.

A mirage in the white heat-haze; battered straw hat, rucksack on back, blue shorts and shirt, staff in his hand. I watched the figure walking down the road; disappearing. Then the flashes of blue shirt between conifer trees in the field, tracking a steady pace; my ears strained at the sounds of noisy climbing over the five-barred gate at the entrance to the home compound. Now the mirage was coming right towards me. Striding up the unsealed driveway towards the house, closer, larger, more focused with each step until Ray was standing right before me, head tilted backward, breathing heavily with exertion, pale blue eyes triumphant behind his glasses.

"Ah ha!" He stopped.

"Hello stranger, and where did you come from?"

At night we slept in the wooden turn-of-the-century bed in my room, which opened onto the front veranda. We made

love, without words. As I imagined the gods made love in the ancient Greek myths. He carried her into the Underworld…
In the days we went off for walks, separately or together. He went off sketching. I walked up the ghost-gum-tangled side of the mountain, up behind the house, gazed across Paradise Plains undulating in the golden late afternoon light.

In the long evenings, we drank red wine on the veranda, as dusk intensified into night's darkness; inhaling the delicious smell of summer earth in the High Country, as the sun goes down, and the air cools at day's end.

Margarita and Raff played oboe and violin in the kitchen. Pieces from Bach's *Art of Fugue,* Margarita had told me rather haughtily. Her smiles, laughter, happy chatter, were only for Raff and Ray. Towards me she was cold, subtly ignoring me in conversations as if trying to make me feel guilty for doing something wrong that she knew about. The others probably didn't notice that she intentionally was cutting me out of the group. Her behaviour affected me, without saying anything to her, I felt torn; I was in a state of conflict. I needed to be on my own, to think or better to not-think, to experience what I needed to know; to make the choice I must.

I set off on long walks.

In the clear light of dawn, I walked up Mount Capricorn loping away from the house through the rows of stunted or dead fruit trees, which the family had referred to as our 'bonsai' orchard: peaches, pears, apricots, plums, pecans, almonds, and apples, all the saplings that had failed to grow as they were supposed to, despite Father's optimistic plans for the variegated orchard, and months, in a family-team, clearing stones, making fields, rabbit-proofing fences. I walked past the dry red pit, which Dad had meant to be a watering pool. It failed to fill after the hired bulldozer dug the hole, because, as we were to find out, the soil was porous, and it wouldn't hold water. All the gallons pumped uphill from the river; designed to fill the dam to the brim, to irrigate the orchard and gardens, had seeped away.

The Farm was a grand family plan that had not come to anything. Instead, it was as if The Farm had become a symbol for the family's unexpected falling apart. Even the term 'Farm', as we called it, turned out to be a cruel misnomer, the land had thwarted taming of the one hundred and fifty hectares of eroded windswept wilderness that—initiated and spurred on by my father— we'd had such grand plans for, and that in only three years made mockeries of all those plans. But I still loved this landscape, and untamed land. I was the only one in the family who still came to the farm, with my friends.

I walked onwards and upwards, following a steep narrow track of red beaten earth, winding through scrubby grass, up over deep gashes of erosion valleys, the ochre earth crumbling and pitted, split open in black jagged zigzags. My feet found a way, kicking aside small pieces of rock and stones that were everywhere, loose sliding scales of a broken skin the arid earth was continually shedding.

The natural land's surface up here in the high country was covered with a layer of grey granite stones softened by green lichens. From the tiniest pebbles to huge boulders protruding monolithically from the earth, the stone crust exposed to constant erosion of wind and sun on treeless land.

I walked through empty forests of stone. Through the thin air of absence, of what once was. I jumped over deep red erosion-gashes, sites of teeming armies of black ants marching in single file. Marching purposefully in the busyness of their lives. Insects exist to remind us of how tiny and futile we are, I thought as I walked: to give us a sense of perspective. What really was the difference to the universe between me and Ray and Margarita, and those ants? They could be fulfilling a cosmically far more valuable role, incomprehensible to the human brain, than we.

Which would not be hard...

My breath came hard and fast as I strode up the mountain, boots slipping and sliding on loose stones and dry grass. I was starting to pant and sweat. The incline was long and steep.

My legs, pumping up the hill, glistened with sweat beneath my cut–off jean shorts. I was wearing a broad brimmed white hat to ward off the ultra-violet rays. I held a stick snapped off from a fallen bough by the creek, a bush pilgrim's staff. It was easier to walk fast with it. My tee-shirt clung stickily to my striding body *Da da daaa da da-da-da-daaa...da da daaa...* ...the rhythm of a song line from Patti Smith's *Horses* repeated through my mind.

I was drenched in sweat. But I wanted it to be hard. Wanted it to hurt. Wanted to push myself as far and fast as I could. I wanted to test the physical limits of pain.

The more it hurt, the more real I felt. Hard exercise was the way I knew to shake off the smothering sense of hopelessness that had fallen over me like a thick blanket.

Watching for snakes, scorpions and spiders, I kept my eyes to the ground and kept going.

I reached the top of the small mountain; we called it the Plateau, which had a radius of about one-kilometre. On the eastern side, it gave way to a thicket of eucalyptus trees, and granite boulders, looking out over Paradise Plains.

This was where I had come to when I wanted to think, or

be on my own: a big flat red boulder, on the edge of a rocky outcrop, by a massive ancient stringy-bark tree. This was the place where I walked to when all the faces, languages, foreign tongues, of people and friends in different countries I'd lived in with the family blurred and roared together, shattering into fragments, when I didn't know which life, who or what to put first, who I was, where I was.

As I headed there, I walked past a brown snake stretched out full length, on a large rock. I knew its venom was deadly. The snake slid away sinuously through the scrubby grass, I walked on in the opposite direction.

I sat on my red rock and looked out over the most perfect view, it reminded me subliminally of a Classical Golden Age pastoral scene—although they were painted before Australia was discovered by Europeans. Beneath a timeless blue-white sky the plains gently undulated in the diffuse early morning light, shimmering incandescently in the building heat. The hazy plains looked made from light, layers of green and gold, stippled mauve shadows, caught purple smudges of trees and bushes adding subtle definition. Rolling away into a radiant horizon from beyond which light emanated.

I gazed as if it could save me from the darkness of confusion: the unknowing, whirling mass of nothingness that filled my mind, when I thought of him, or her. I longed to find answers in my gazing. No answers came. I gazed and gazed, and it all seemed just as confused, as incomprehensible as ever.

As I walked downhill to the house, I heard them, before I saw Margy and Raff tuning their instruments in the kitchen.

I painted all morning to the sounds of musical fugues being practiced in the house. Raymond set off to do some sketching. We seemed to be moving into separate spaces in the daytime, unlike Margarita and her great friend Raffles (gay) whom J. S. Bach did bond. With musical bars and lines of flight.

When Ray came back I walked out from my room and met him on the front porch.

"Let's go into the bedroom," I extended my hand, touched his arm. It seemed a long way from me to him. I had made a decision.

He followed me. I sat on my bed. He stood on the striped Greek rug. The door was half open, framing the molten light. Silence fell like a void between us, and it wasn't a quiet tranquil silence, it was deafening as the shrieking midday screech of cicadas.

"I'm going back to Adelaide with Margarita," I said at last. "We're going to get an apartment together."

Everything seemed suddenly clear, defined by the sharpness of my words. The country so close outside my room: blinding white-green grassy paddocks, pale-green fountains of rogue willow trees, seen through my window, distorted in the purple and yellow panes in the upper and lower sections. Samuel had found the colonial windows after a holiday-house by the river blew down in a severe storm. He'd carried them back despite their awkward weight and bulk, and replaced the aluminium frames that had been there before.

"Yeah, right sport," Ray said. He sounded tired. "I'm going to get a drink." He wandered off across the porch and through the open living room door. A minute or so later, the music squeaking and soaring through the heat suddenly stopped. I could hear Margarita's excited treble voice, swooping and spiralling into laughter. Despite the hostility she expressed to me, she didn't seem to have any problems talking to Raymond. Then Raff's complementary treble, his high pitched laughter.

Raff's peals of laughter that harmonised with the entry of Ray's tenor cackle.

I lay on my back on the nineteenth-century colonial double bed, with its embossed carving of an urn on the bedhead for company. Margarita seemed to be doing such a great job of entertaining, I thought. I'll leave her to it.

As soon as Ray left, he was gone. I had no way of contacting him, knowing what he was doing, where he was, where he was going next; I started missing him. Longing for him again…

I kept my feelings to myself. But I knew that it was not over. It couldn't be over, not when I felt like this.

The next day I was poisoned. In order to save the kilometre walk to our stretch of the river and back up the steep hillside, I suggested that we take some water from the next-door neighbour's water tank. Jayden Larty used his place as an occasional holiday house. There was seldom anyone there. We'd been walking through his property, to the best swimming pool—a bend in the river sheltered by a ridge on one side and shaded by old-growth gums and willows, which was easier to get to by walking directly over his land, than by walking along the Murrumbidgee meandering through our property, the riverbanks at the boundary were overgrown with tea tree, briar rose, brambles and tussocks. Jayden said we could walk over his land, and sometimes we did.

We'd been walking right past the shed Jayden had done-up as his holiday house, and I'd noticed a water tank outside. A 40-gallon drum, on bricks, with a tap fixed into the base. That afternoon, we'd decided to take some water from his tank.

"By the time he's down next it's sure to have rained and refilled anyway," I assured the others.

It was a very hot afternoon. There was no shade on the way from our place to Jayden's. We returned carrying filled flagons; all of us streaming with sweat. We reached the kitchen, and put down the flagons on the old food cupboard that doubled as a bench top.

"I feel like I'm burning up!" I wiped my forehead with my shirt. I filled a cup first. I drank five or six glasses of water, one after the other, hardly pausing to take a breath.

I felt queasy. Maybe one of us should have tasted the water before drinking it in quantity?

The stomach pains began about twenty minutes later.

Pain was soon an understatement for what I was feeling. Delirious, in agony, rolling on my bed, gasping, writhing, my body was rapidly expelling hot waves of perspiration. I couldn't see properly. I was aware of Margarita and Raff, murmuring in alarm above me. I couldn't feel the flannel Margarita was pressing to my brow.

Then they were gone and I was alone.

Twisting and groaning with pain, fireballs exploded in my eyes; burning, stabbing, shooting pain ripped my guts apart.

I was dying.

Margarita returned.

"I've packed up everything," my friend's voice reached me as if from a long distance—the land of normality and health. I could barely hear or make sense of her words.

She helped me into a sitting position, her arms around my back and shoulders. Every movement amplified the cramps. I staggered bent double between her and Raff as they helped me out of my room.

"We're going back to Canberra," said Margarita.

"It's just as well you came down," I heard her say to Raff,

who managed a cheery giggle, despite my imminent demise.

We reached the edge of the town, the sign of Cooma.

"I have to go to the loo," I said weakly. Raff swerved into a petrol service station. Cheerful bright yellow-and-green lights, manic neon, cut my optic nerves, sharp daggers exploding my tunnel vision. Bent double, groaning, I just made it into the 'rest room'.

I don't know how long I was in there. The pain did not diminish. I staggered back to the car. Raff held the door open and I fell onto the back seat, collapsed in a sealed capsule of laceration and torment, as we sped off down the Highway.

We arrived back in Glebe around midnight. Mum was not there. Where am I?

"That's right, she said she was going to a conference in Brisbane," Margarita said behind me as I staggered through the laundry.

"She said she wouldn't be back until the 25th, that's three days away." Margarita was always so efficient; she knew these things. I crawled along the hallway to my bedroom and threw myself onto the bottom bunk, which is where I stayed hardly moving except for feverish thrashing for the next days. I thought that I was in a big house with several stories, or storeys, in a capital city.

"No we're not in Sydney, we're in your Mum's house."

That didn't seem to make any sense/we must be in Beijing.

The pain and delirium continued for days. I had feverish dreams of Margarita looking after me. Holding damp flannels to my brow. Bringing me water that I sipped from a teaspoon. Gradually the poison was flushed from my system.

As I recovered, I heard her playing, the music floating up the stairs from the bungalow dining room.

The sweet melodic soaring of her violin,
tearing through the mornings and the afternoons,
quivering on the edges of my departing delirium.

The notes of her ascending footsteps, mounting the stairs, towards me, her voice, which I was so glad to hear:

"How are you feeling? Are you any better? Can I get you anything? Some dry biscuits? A cup of tea?"

The pains have gone, I am delirious. I am feeling very weak. At night, in absent mother's house, Margarita sleeps in my bed. To keep watch. Drifting into restless sleep; drift, dream and drift—

In the daytime, in high fever, I am at her mercy, subjugated by caring, concern. A patient.

We are heading together, unknowing and unknown, into the shadowy lands of the Haunted Castle. It is calling to us from the future and it shall find us. It shall possess us and consume us; there is no other way.

Margy and I sat on the front porch, gazing towards the embankment sloping up to the road, lazily watching the late-afternoon traffic. I was drinking white wine, and she G and T's. Margarita liked to play the colonial lady with her quinine and her parasol. We were talking about the perennial question…

"Oh! What shall we do???" I beseeched, gesturing dramatically.

"I'll only go with you if I know you're not going to get back with Raymond," she said.

I thought that was a bit of a tall order.

"I'm not going to a place where I don't know anyone, and have to play the wallflower. It's all right for you; you lived there with Samuel, last year. You know people." Her high-pitched voice vibrated insistently, in the heat of the languid afternoon.

Resonant as the ringing tone produced by my wine-moist middle finger encircling the rim of the crystal glass. I poured another to soften its cutting demands.

Raymond. Ray, unofficial leader of neo-Dada art-activists, the Art Scandals, and conceptual artist, had been my boyfriend since the beginning of summer. I had been in not-love. But that was all in the past now.

"You needn't worry, it's over between us," I assured her, staring down a blue sedan cruising past.

"More vidka, my dear?" I tipped glittering liquid into her glass. Margarita drank Polish vodka, Polka.

The lines from a half-forgotten Japanese poem drifted, tantalizingly, through the air, but I decided not to say them out loud. She probably wouldn't know it, anyway.

"Damn, no ice," she said, looking into the jug. "I'm going to go and get some." She walked indoors.

Quickly, I picked up the bag at my feet. In it was a photo concealed in my notebook, one of the ones taken at the Farm, which came back from the developers the day before. I slipped it out and stared at it.

Raymond and I, standing on the steps of the veranda; I'm on the top step; under the overhang of the veranda roof, hair up in a high ponytail. My shadowy profile turned away from the lens is dark, cool, brooding: eyes half-closed, unfocussed, gazing into a private realm of inner space. Raymond, on the step below, is caught in the full glare of the mid-day sun. His sharp-featured face is radiant in the white light. Old canvas backpack slung over his shoulders, clear rims of his glasses held together by sticky-tape. His head tilted at a rakish angle, beneath a straw hat. He is staring at the camera, at Margarita taking the photo, with an inscrutably blank expression on his pink face. He is setting out on a walk... A sketching expedition... In his backpack, watercolours, sketchbook...

"God, I just don't know what to do..." Margy said loudly, stepping onto the front porch. I dropped the photo back into my bag and shoved it under my chair. Since she'd dropped out of her photography B.A. in Melbourne her inner turmoil was escalating to a climax. "I'm fed-up with witnessing."

"Well, I'm not surprised," I said. I watched a station wagon followed by a jeep. I had lost every waitressing job I'd ever had, usually after the trial session.

"I'm thinking about taking up classical violin again. You know I played in the School Orchestra until I was thirteen. That is, until just before I met you," she said. *Not this again!*

"Daddy taught me to play violin from when I was only three," she continued petulantly.

I looked at her musician's fingers draped elegantly around the stem of Isobel's new bohemian crystal goblet. I thought of Margy's manic geometry when she was playing her improvised music.

"But your electric violin!" I protested.

"It's brilliant! You must stick with it!"

It was celebration music. I'd watched her on stage in the spotlight, playing with the band, in her black silk slip.

"How could you think of giving that up?"

She was taking little sips of her drink, sighing to herself, as if she knew things that were way beyond my understanding.

But I, at least, knew what I was doing. I was returning to Adelaide to begin Second Year of my Arts degree. And I had no one to go with.

I couldn't stop thinking about Raymond. *Trying to find something rare, so beautiful no one will believe it can exist... You confuse me but I love it...* But I couldn't tell her that.

"I'm never going to see him again," I took a deep satisfying swig, draining my glass.

"Anyway," I reached for the bottle. "It's not as if I'm going to get the chance, he's going off to paint in the Tropics. When he leaves his cousin's place, he said he's going north to Cairns, then further north out of the country. He said he'd end up in Papua New Guinea, like that painter we were talking about." I laughed brightly.

"Gauguin didn't go to PNG," said Margarita tightly. "He went to Tahiti."

As if I didn't know that. But I always humoured Margarita, despite her bossiness and forthright ways. It was part of the unspoken pact of our friendship.

"You do know what I mean... And if I did see him, I'd just ignore him anyway," I reassured her.

Reggie's Rooms

The boarding house was the only accommodation we'd been able to find—we'll be lucky, I assured Margarita—after a long sweltering afternoon, lost in labyrinths of streets that activated thrilling memories for me, but which did not hold the same significance (or any) for her. We toiled, in our quest, through the maze of backstreets, walking in the relentless sunlight. Saddled with backpacks, and carrying multiple bags, straining arms, bumping legs, impeding progress, like rocks in a kayakers' stream. The sun blazed; Margarita said she felt nauseous. I was light-headed, and it wasn't just the heat.

I was here again, in Adelaide, in the streets leading to the enchanted fairground of Raymond's hometown. Although he'd said he was planning to travel, I hoped against hope that he would return to Adelaide (he'd need to get his passport!). After all, he thought that I was coming back here...

Everyone from Rubicon Road had scattered at the end of the college year. We'd gone separate ways, without exchanging telephone numbers, which of course most of us did not have. Without Samuel, I was hardly going to go to Tony's.

"Don't worry. I remember there're lots of places to rent.

There's a notice-board in a shop, where I lived last year, with accommodation vacant notices—we'll go there."

When we got off the tram at Glenelg, I'd found the supermarket and the noticeboard. The advertisements on the old corkboard in the shop entrance were not of the kind that I remembered.

"Home repairs?" "Learn to Sail??'" Margy snapped. "There isn't one apartment here!"

"Let's walk around and have a look. We'll find something—people put notices in their windows, remember it's a holiday place, people let out rooms, and their flats and houses."

I picked up my baggage, putting on an upper crust British accent.

"Come on! Hop-Two! That's the spirit!"

I had no idea where to go, but I thought if we walked up the main street, and headed left above the block where I lived last year, we were bound to see a house with a Vacancy notice in the window.

We started walking and kept on, for hours, through the streets. Margarita decided to conserve energy by not talking. Up, down, across, over the flat avenues, roads and closes that all looked the same. We walked in silence past red brick villas, and white painted bungalows, with a garage next to the house, a front path, a wall or a fence, palm tress and tall stiff fronds of vegetation in the front garden. No Vacancy notices to be seen only No Vacancies. Maybe we could sleep in the sand dunes at the end of Glenelg Beach, I thought for a moment before dismissing the idea, I was not with Samuel now.

In the heat of the long afternoon, we walked up and down, around and around, until my ears were ringing, and vision swimming. I had an imaginary hallucination of suburbia, a hideous mirage. All houses, no people visible, dripping and melting together, merging into the One House, the prototypical bungalow, that we were destined to walk past forever; like mice, spinning on a treadmill, unable to make any progress, in the glittering heat of the endless afternoon. Trapped in time.

"It'll be okay." I had to keep talking. Communication was a lifeline to hope. Or was it the other way around?

"We'll have to find something soon."

We passed a steamy launderette.

A huge gasping woman stood in the open doorway, sweat dripping down her mottled mauve-grey cheeks.

"There's someone! Let's ask her!"

"Excuse me," I ventured. "I don't suppose you know of any places to rent around here?"

"You could try Reggie's Rooms, it's round the next corner," she began to wheeze.

"That sounds like what we're looking for!" I smiled, turning to Margarita. She didn't look well. Under her broad-brimmed black hat her face was scarlet and dripping with sweat.

"I need water." She broke her silence.

We stopped, put down our stuff. I rummaged in my army surplus bag for the bottles.

"Here!" I passed her one.

She drank.

I drank. We readjusted our backpacks and picked up the loose bags. Margy was clutching the handle of her violin case as if it were a miniature suitcase. Slowly we walked, turning at the corner, into another street that looked exactly like the one before.

"Why didn't we notice this?" I asked as we stood outside a tall once-grand white house.

"Probably because we didn't come down this street."

"Exactly!"

Sitting on the flight of steps to the front door of the house, a grey-haired, grey-faced man smoked a cigarette.

"Excuse me," I squinted up at him.

"Yaars?" he exhaled, looking down at us.

"Is this Reggie's Rooms?"

"Yaars," he inhaled, looking away.

"Do you know where we could find Reggie?" I asked.

I rang the bell. There was no response. I kept ringing. After a few minutes, a middle-aged man dressed in a blue-and-white striped sailing top, white trousers, deck-shoes, and peaked cap opened the door suddenly. He looked very startled to see us.

"Are you Reggie?" I asked.

"Yes." We'd followed the grey man's directions correctly.

"We heard that you might have a flat to let?"

"There is one available, you're in luck!" His expression was slightly flustered and the tone of his voice was obliging. Reggie was English; he had smooth skin and a politely worried demeanour. He kept smiling anxiously, as he took us up to the empty second-floor apartment.

"Here it is!" he said as he unlocked the door, and stepped back so we could enter. There was one big room with a bed, a wardrobe and a table. French doors opened onto a covered-in balcony with windows converting it into a room that housed a kitchen with a small bed built into the end wall, concealed by a curtain.

"You'll have to share the bathroom." Reggie was smiling even more anxiously, his face breaking out into beads of sweat.

"Where is the bathroom?" I said.

"With each other?" Margy asked at exactly the same time.

"The house," he coughed.

"Oh, that's okay," I said. "We don't mind that."

"Oh no, not at all," Margy said sarcastically. "We just love sharing bathrooms."

I elbowed her in the ribs, and glared at her to shut up. Did she want to sleep on the beach?

"It's on the far side of the upper hall," Reggie answered my question. "Just over the hall from this apartment."

"I'll let you have a look around by yourselves. I'll be down in my office. If you want to decide to take it come down and let me know and we can fix it up. You can move in now."

After he had disappeared from view, and earshot, we paced over to the bathroom.

"At least it's reasonably clean."

Margarita snorted in derision.

"What do you think?" I asked.

"What's the alternative?"

"Well, isn't this lucky?" I said, as we closed the door of our new abode.

"Like winning the lottery."

We paced around the gloomy room.

I became aware of an unpleasant odour. Like a nauseating compound of centuries-old underarm perspiration with base notes of rotting vegetation; it was like granulated dirt that had crumbled to dust... Margarita sneezed.

"God, the place stinks," she said. "And it's very dark in this room, those old doors opening onto the balcony let in hardly any light!"

"I can do something about that!" I walked across the carpet.

"Let there be light!" I flicked the light switch by the door.

Margarita rolled her eyes. At least I could see her.

With the light on, the room looked even more dingy and desolate.

"Hmm, we'll have to get a lamp..." I said.

"Who's going to have which room?"

"Let's toss a coin."

I extracted a twenty-cent piece from my wallet, and shook it in my cupped hands.

It was only after I unpacked my backpack and was arranging notepads and pens on the table that I realized I could not see my most precious possession. After I'd looked over the bags on the floor and rifled through their contents I was struck by a belated feeling of dread.

"Margy! Is my typewriter in your room?"

She had carried her bags into the balcony space and was setting up a small dressing table on a chair next to a tiny bed space, built into the wall.

"No!" she called back a few moments later.

"Where is it?" I wailed.

Frantically I checked again through the bags.

"It's not here!!"

"If you left it at the railway station or on the train it should be in Lost Property."

"I'll go and ring them now—I remember passing a phone box outside that launderette. Are you coming?"

"It's a bit late—it's almost eight-o' clock. They'll be closed probably. Why don't we just go there tomorrow?"

"There'll be people there—it's a train station— Adelaide is a city. It should be open shouldn't it?"

"I doubt it, but I'll come with you."

We set out on our first sortie away from our new lodgings, retracing our steps in the golden light of evening, back to the launderette where the wheezing woman had pointed the way to a place to stay, and our new life here. While Margy waited outside the phone box, I dialled Directory Enquiries, got the Lost Property number, and rang it. After what seemed like an age it rang out.

"They're closed."

"What did I tell you?"

"God. God. God. Damn. Damn. Damn. I don't believe it. How could I have lost it? How could I have left it on the train or on the platform? I need it! I do all my writing on it!"

"It's probably there, Roxy. Don't think about it till we go there tomorrow."

"I just don't believe I could have missed it when we were transporting all our stuff."

"Shall we see if there's any shops open, to get something to eat for dinner?"

"I'm not hungry. But okay."

I couldn't think about food due to the anxiety my missing typewriter was causing me. We walked to the end of the street onto Jetty Road, crossed over the tram tracks and kept walking down the street almost to the sea, the jetty, and the tall marble monument topped with a sailing ship commemorating the founding of the city settlement by free settlers. Before us was the open vista of Holdfast Bay darkening now with approaching night.

"Let's just have the cheese and biscuits we brought with us," I said. "We don't have much money anyway."

We bought green apples and a carton of milk at an Italian

café, and returned to the new rooms.

Early next morning, after eating bowls of the muesli we'd brought with us, and each having a shower and washing hair, we set out to the train station. Margy was sporting a blue and green 1950s frock with a full skirt and black belt, a black wide brimmed hat and her tap dancing shoes with ankle socks. I was wearing my old army surplus trousers, a purple vest under a pink blouse, and a black hat and round sunglasses, carrying my army shoulder bag. We walked out into a hot summer day.

We caught the tram at Moseley Square opposite the jetty. To the south, the sun shone on the glittering expanse of the water of the Bay covering it with a patina of radiant light; above, the clear blue sky stretched infinitely. We embarked. The number 368 clanked and whirred down Jetty Road flanked by shops and cafés. In front of us the Adelaide hills rose high and blue on the northern horizon. The tram rocked and swayed, with a dinging of its bell into the City, passing South Terrace, we reached the colonial building of the Railway Station in North Terrace, where we disembarked.

We walked into the station. Lost Property was located near the front.

The whole journey there I had been tense and nervous with anticipation and dread, and my usually optimistic nature managed to muster only a modicum of hope. I practiced my yoga breathing to stay calm.

I approached the counter in the nineteenth-century room, in the annexe open to the public, behind which was a portal into the catacombs of lost things. A bearded man in a blue uniform stood on the other side. He looked up from what he was doing as we walked in.

"Hi. I caught the train from Melbourne to Adelaide arriving

yesterday late afternoon, and have discovered that my portable typewriter is missing. I think it might have been accidentally left on the train or on the platform. Has it been handed in, please?"

"A portable typewriter?" He repeated.

"Yes."

He turned and walked through the portal behind him.

He returned a few minutes later.

"Can't see anything there," he said.

He turned to a ledger on a shelf, and looked over a couple of pages carefully.

"No, nothing has come in."

"Oh no."

"But it could be handed in over the next weeks. It can take a while for things left on the train to turn up."

"Okay thanks, I'll come back and check."

We walked out into blinding sunlight.

I sighed deeply.

"Damn. Bloody hell. How could I have left it on the train?"

"Let's go for a walk through the Rundle Mall," Margy said.

As we were walking in the city we passed an antiques bric-a-brac shop, and went inside. I found an old piano accordion, in fine working order. When I was a child I'd had a toy piano accordion, which I learnt to play, and loved. This was a real one, with a decorative maroon panel above the keys.

"It's a beauty," the shop owner said.

I picked it up and imagined myself in my red gypsy dress— accompanying Margy on violin.

After deliberating for a while, I put a twenty-dollar deposit on it.

Maybe I had found a new kind of keyboard to play on.

But, as things were to turn out, I was never to collect the instrument.

Reggie, quite properly, had not said anything about the other tenants. It was a surprise to find it was a men's boarding house. I saw them in the corridors of the big dark house. We passed them on the stairs, or in the front hallway, on our way to the shops or beach. Or I would pass them as I walked, holding my wash-bag, to and from the bathroom. At first, I thought it was the same person: a thin stooping middle-aged grey man with a cigarette and a smoker's cough.

After I'd seen this vision in duplicate, or even triplicate, talking together in the hallway or outside the house, I realized that all the men in the boarding house looked alike. Shuffling about in white vest, baggy trousers, walking up and down the stairs, puffing, wheezing, coughing, trailing hazy grey plumes of smoke. There appeared to be no other female occupants.

The grey men looked kind of embarrassed mingled with curious, as we walked past them on the stairs, or in the foyer.

"They give me the creeps, they're like ghosts or shadows..." said Margarita.

"Should we say hello, or what?" I said.

"Don't start talking to them—we don't want anyone to get the wrong idea."

Margarita had lost the toss when we moved in. With a flip of a twenty-cent piece, "Tails!" I won, and chose the big room, furnished with the sagging double bed, which was carefully made with sheets and blankets (to be replaced immediately by Samuel's good-quality sleeping bag). A dark wardrobe loomed towards the ceiling; I moved it to the foot of my bed, to give more space, which turned my bed into an alcove.

"It looks like the wardrobe in *The Tenant*," Margarita said as we gingerly took stock of our new abode. Now, whenever I looked at the wardrobe, an uneasy image from the horror film disturbed my thoughts; the transsexual in make-up; gibbering quietly inside, biding time, waiting to leap out at us, when we least expected it.

The wardrobe was the last thing in my line of sight before I went to sleep, towering in front of me, holding clothes, shoes and hats, all our things mixed up together. I had to deliberately turn my head to not notice it; and after switching off the bedside lamp I'd bought, I carefully turned and looked away before I closed my eyes.

With my lucky flip, I had won the large dark wooden table in my room; I pictured myself arranging painting things on the table, creating a studio. But the day after we moved in, Margy started practicing in the big room. "Can't you play in the kitchen?" I asked her. "Couldn't you practice in there?"

She curled her lip in a ravishing expression of contempt.

"Roxy. For goodness sake, I'm practicing for my audition. For the Conservatorium," she hissed passionately.

Margarita was unattractive when disdainful: head thrown back, full lips quivering with scorn.

"There's no room to sit down, let alone play violin in the so-called 'kitchen.'"

As she said the word "kitchen," she hooked her two index fingers into the shape of wiggling mocking "scare-quotes."

"Can you take this seriously?" Her high-pitched voice rose until it was ringing in my ears.

I looked at her. I knew how important this was for her. I

thought about her family. Ghosts of tortures, terrible histories, hovered in the boarding room's stagnant air. At that moment there was nothing that seemed more important in the whole world, than that Margy play the family instrument.

"Okay, then. Fine."

With Margarita playing in my room I wasn't able to paint in there. I had to abandon my notes and research for my next year's university essays on the table—behind Margarita's metronome and self-help books. I kept my anxiety to myself, and shifted into the kitchenette.

One night, so late it felt as if the apartment had turned into a dream around me, I painted Margarita, as I had seen her that day from my position in the balcony-room, in the house. The floor sloped slightly yet noticeably at a downward angle away from the main building. It felt alarmingly as if, if you jumped, the balcony-room could crash into the luxuriant garden below. Everything was doll-size, scaled-down, miniature. There was a shaky card-table, and a one-ring gas stove. Margarita's bed, concealed behind ragged green and yellow was on a wide shelf built widthways against the wall. A child-size bunk bed in an Eastern European gypsy caravan; she had to curl up her legs to fit onto it.

I slid my brush, down her white, muscular arms. I rolled dots, streaks of white, into a ghostly luminescence. Painting from life, I stroked the edges of her pale heart-shaped face.

Her eyes large, languorous, heavy-lidded, iridescent blue, fringed with black lashes. Irish eyes. I chose intense cerulean. Added a touch of white to lighten it just a bit. Stroked each dark lash with the delicate tip of my sable brush. Her nose was aquiline. A shadow of grey indicated its presence. I had to get this right...

Her features quivered with the refinement and complexity of the music. She'd told me once it was 'Baroque' as opposed to 'classical.' It was the kind of music grandparents listened to. The music I liked listening to was post-punk Patti Smith... I wasn't getting a chance to play my tapes now.

"At least one of us is still in touch with the modern world." I said only half-joking.

Margarita had renounced her electric violin, her music; wild sweet improvised psychedelic mazurkas she had played with Tiimon's art-punk band in Melbourne. I had danced to her manic music, busking with her on inner-city streets. I couldn't understand why she had chosen to give up her art, the music that came from her soul. She was already known as an avant-garde sound artist and now she was giving that up. But she hadn't listened to me.

"Margarita, could you please take a break. I'd rather hear something different, I'm trying to write an essay in here," I implored her from the balcony-room.

"Roxy, I've told you, I've got to get it right for my audition. No, I can't stop."

"Okay then. Fine. In that case, I'm going out." Slam!

As time passed, my friend and I were fast becoming locked in a silent—or, rather, non-verbalized—battle of style wars. Unspoken divisions splintered between the high squeaks and jarring discords.

Every morning when I got up I brewed strong coffee and sat at the tiny table in the kitchenette. Legs jammed against the fibro wall, I gazed through dusty old windowpanes into tangled undergrowth. I gazed out at the early autumn sky. But I couldn't focus on the scenery. All I saw, in my mind, was he.

My secret thoughts about him since I'd left him in the rainforest had started off in a plaintive trickle. Now they were developing into an uncontrollable rushing torrent.

I couldn't stop missing him. Dreaming about him day and night. Was I dreaming him or was he dreaming me? Was I picking up some psychic rays of his desire? Or would I really never see him again? It just didn't seem possible it was over. Not as I still felt this way. I had kept my desire for him secret but that seemed to only make my longing stronger.

It was a blue clear-skied afternoon. We had walked to Brighton Jetty along the beach, five miles, eight k's, and were walking from Brighton beach to the esplanade when she saw him. A wrenchingly familiar figure dressed in black, sloping past the bottle shop on the far side of the road.

"Look who it isn't," Margarita grabbed my arm.

"Furnett!!" she shouted. Furnett?? Why so familiar? *What maketh thee so bold my dear?* After all the things she'd said, that she didn't want me to have anything to do with him?

He turned, looked around, then saw us and raised his hand.

Margarita and I walked up from the sand. Ray crossed the road.

We met on the pavement above the beach. Later I thought of it in geometric terms, which descended into a romantic cliché. The three of us meeting in a glittering triangle of hope, despair, and desire. Like three Shakespearian witches plucking words to make a spell, which of we three would be the most powerful? Whose desire, whose will, would prevail? Excitement and danger crackled in the air like sulphur mingled with salt. I looked into his blue eyes and felt myself starting to fall.

It was Margarita who gave Ray our new address.

The next day when Margy and I returned from the beach, she unlocked the door and screamed.

"Oh God, what's that, Oh God...God..." Her voice went very quiet. She sounded genuinely scared.

"What, what is it," I hissed behind her.

"No," she whispered in horror. "Go back! I don't think we should be going in, I don't know what it is but—It's something very weird. Go back, go out..."

"What? why?" I walked in, squeezing past her, and stood looking around.

On the floor in the doorway between the rooms there was an album: a vinyl record in a cover.

"What is it?" she whispered.

"It's a record," I said.

"Yes, but where's it come from, we don't have any records."

"There must be someone here?" She whispered in a tone of horror.

"Hello!" I called out. "Hello!"

There was no sound. I walked quickly towards the French doors, and peered into the balcony room.

"There's no-one here," I said.

Margarita was standing next to the wardrobe.

With a quick determined movement she swung around, and pulled the doors open.

"And there's no-one in there," she said, as if it was a comedy routine.

"There's nowhere else anyone could be," I said. She looked at me theatrically, pointing at my bed. Mouthing the words:

What about??

I bent and looked under the bed. "No-one there. I don't know how anyone could fit there anyway with the backpacks and bags and cases."

"What about on my bed," she hissed. "Behind the curtains."

"No. I just looked. The curtain's open. There's nothing on your bed."

She had walked up to the album and stood staring down at it as it were radioactive.

"What is it?" I asked.

"It's a record, I thought we'd decided that."

"I mean what record, who's the artist?"

She bent down and picked it up.

"Throbbing Offal," she read in a mystified tone.

"That's a band Ray was talking about."

"Ray. Could it have something to do with Ray? Could he have put it here? But how could he get in? It's impossible."

She gazed around helplessly, shrugging.

"The lock is quite secure. He couldn't have come in here."

"What about the balcony windows?"

We walked into the little room. There was a window open next to the table.

"Could anyone get through there?" I said.

"No. It's impossible. Have a look. It's the first floor, there isn't even a wall to scale," Margy said.

"This is really weird." I said.

Neither of us felt like sitting down and having a coffee or tea. We kept pacing around the flat, restlessly.

"I'm not sure if I want to stay here now," she said. "This is really spooky."

"I agree," I said. "It's strange, like there's a goddamn ghost in here or something."

"Oh don't say that," she said, "Now I'm starting to get the chills. It's reminding me of *that film*, more and more. Oh God, this place is giving me the creeps, why did we move in here?"

"Yeah," I said. "I feel completely freaked out. This is really, really odd."

"I mean? It's a bizarre thing: a record in the middle of the flat. Not even on the table," she said.

"Hmm."

"Shall we go out, go into the city, to that wholefood café in Rundle Mall? Then go to One-Not-One, there'll be a band tonight—it's Thursday."

"Yeah, okay. Let's get out of here for a while."

I put on my new vintage red dress, which I called my gypsy dress. The dress was mid-calf length with a full circular skirt, a tight fitting bodice, and a square neckline trimmed with white broderie anglaise. I'd found it in the Melbourne markets, with Margarita. Tried it on squeezed between racks of dresses and coats smelling of musty old wardrobes and decay.

"Doesn't she look something?" The mature, worldly-wise woman running the stall had said to Margarita, as I stood out from the mass of clothes, and tried to gain some perspective looking into a mirror with a speckled surface.

"Yes," said Margarita.

"She's so slim!" the woman said. They exchanged glances.

"I know!!" said Margy, "it's sickening!"

The joke had an edge, as they rolled their eyes and emitted exaggerated sighing noises. I felt like an outsider.

I'd noticed that the market-woman was wearing black eye liner, lipstick and a leopard-skin coat over a black dress. Her bouffant hairdo was streaked blonde and bronze. When Margy spoke to her she talked with familiarity, laughing, bantering. I held back. What could I say.

"Well, I think I will get it," I had said slowly, after weighing up the price. I liked the colour, and clean lines, and thought it would be good to dance in, with the circular skirt.

The red gypsy dress reminded me of freedom, made me think of whirling tango dancers, Spanish lovers drinking wine in a bar as the sun goes down and guitars strum softly—words I wrote in a notebook when I was much younger and tried to express what I felt when I heard guitar music. I had always loved music and dancing.

I put on my black low-heeled ankle boots. I was starting to think about wearing make-up again. I had bought some white powder in the local costume shop, plum-purple lipstick, from a chemist on the high street. I peered into the circular shaving mirror on the table, lightly dusted my face with powder, and smeared my lips with the lippie. Now my eyes were too pale, receding in the mask-like effect of my white face.

"Margy—can I borrow your black eyeliner?"

"Eyeliner! Shure, ye're not getting made up?" She exclaimed in her Ballyweaver accent, as she came walking into my room, in black bra and tight black satin trousers.

"You're not actually going to wear those?" I grimaced at the choice she'd made in the markets.

She put the eyeliner on the table.

"Yes, of course I am, why not?" she retorted, and disappeared back into her room.

She soon reappeared, sporting the rest of her ensemble, a yellow and black satin oriental top, and her black tap dancing shoes. Her hair was braided in a single plait that hung almost to her waist; face white and lips vermilion.

"You look like a mime artist, Marcella!" I teased.

We caught the tram, arriving at Lettice's wholefood restaurant in the Mall, as the evening sky turned dark. We sat down at a table by the window.

"What are you having?" Margarita said, in the airy green-walled room, looking at the menu.

"I'm not sure, I'm not very hungry actually."

"It's alright," she said. "I'm going to have the adzuki bean pie and nasturtium salad, followed by carrot cake with carob icing. Forget the diet, I've not had a good meal for ages!"

"I think I'll just have a macrobiotic salad. I'm dying for a coffee."

"By the way, did you know that we are living in a palindrome?" I said, as we waited for our orders to arrive.

"What are you on about?"

"Glenelg. G-L-E-N-E-L-G if you spell it backwards, it's the same."

I gazed out at the empty street.

"Oh yes," said Margy, laughing. "So it is."

"It's strange you know. When I first moved to Glenelg last year, and Samuel and I moved into the house with Margarita and Lily, that was like a kind of palindrome."

"What do you mean?"

"They reflected you and Lily, same names, same hair colour. They were different ages though."

"It's not a palindrome—we weren't the same as them. And they weren't exactly mine and Lily's names spelt backwards!"

"No, you're right." I was troubled by the idea. There was something disturbing about concepts of doubling, and self-reflectivity, like looking at one's reflection in a box of mirrors, going on forever. It looks like one but is not one.

After dinner, we went to One-Not-One; a punk-art band, that I had seen last year with Samuel, was playing. We walked there; the punk venue was in a street off Hindley Street in a couple of large ground floor rooms in a Victorian pub. As we turned the corner into the street I could feel the vibrations of the music emanating from the pub half-way down the narrow lane. The three-chord thrash, binary thump, of punk music: the sound of the times. At the door, collecting entry fees was Ray's friend, Frankie. Immediately, my nervous system lit up. Was Ray here?

"Good evening," I said handing Frankie a note. He smiled at me.

"Hi Frank," said Margy. I was surprised she knew his name.

The room was three-quarters full, I glanced around quickly, there were several people I knew from art parties and gigs. No sign of Ray. We stood at the edge of the room where the band was.

I felt anxious and restless.

As if I sensed her intention Margy rotated onto the dance floor. There were people dancing, but not like her. She began to twirl and gyrate in a manic style, almost as if on the verge of a fit. Her body looked rigid as she did her intuitive tap-dancing, arms akimbo and fingers splayed. She almost looked as if she were being electrocuted. Ever since the faulty wiring in the garage I'd lived in, in Canberra, had given me an electric shock when I turned on the electric jug with washing-up wet hands that had thrown me backwards and left a black burn on my finger, I'd been uncomfortably aware of electric shocks. I noticed that Ray's friends were glancing at her with inscrutable looks on their faces.

Neither of us was drinking alcohol. I sipped water; when the next song started, an anthem to callow youth, I joined her on the dance floor. Not that she gave any acknowledgment to my presence. We danced for the whole set. Ray did not show up.

When the music stopped, she said: "Let's go and say hello."

"What? To whom?"

"To Ray's friends over there."

I winced at her forwardness; she hadn't even lived here last year. She didn't know them.

"Um, I don't think so, they're not like that."

"Oh come on, Love," she said.

I demurred, "I only really know Ray, not all of his friends."

"Come on, we can say we're on the way to the bar!"

She rushed ahead. I followed her to Ray's friends, grouped together at the side of the room, Tel sitting on the floor, Dog standing.

Tel, in a black leather jacket, red vest, blue leather trousers, was with a guy with a studded collar around his neck, wearing eyeliner, white face, gothic make-up; and a girl with cropped black hair, in a black bin-liner dress cinched at the waist with several narrow strips of canvas.

Dog was wearing a black leather jacket, ripped jeans and a tartan shirt, and his blonde hair was slicked back.

"Hi!" said Margy breezily.

Tel looked up at us.

"Uh hi," said Dog.

"Do you remember me?" Margarita smiled. I looked away, did she have to do this? "I was staying in Adelaide last winter, and we were at that theatre performance in the car park, with Ray! I've moved up here now."

"Uh, yeah," said Dog.

"So Ray's not around?" she said loudly.

"Nah."

"Oh well, good to see you, we're on our way to the bar!"

I smiled ruefully. We walked to the bar. I needed a drink.

"White wine, thanks."

We returned after midnight. Warily walking into the flat, we immediately looked to see if any other unusual items had appeared on the floor, but all seemed as we left it. After tiring ourselves out dancing, at least I could fall asleep, without fear, in my bed.

Yet the mystery of the vinyl record remained unsolved, and in my dreams I had disturbing visions of a clown character with red hair and red nose, spinning records as Margy whirled like a robot, a machine-girl on a dance floor slowly filling with green water.

The next day, some time, in the hazy late noon, when I was writing, and Margarita reading on her bed, I heard the ascending footsteps, and then a firm knock-knock on the door.

"What's that?" Margy called from the balcony-room.

"Who is it?" I called out loudly.

"You have a visitor!" replied a muffled familiar voice.

My heart sped and I felt I could not breathe.

I stood up, breathing in deeply, and went to open the door.

"Ha-ha-ha—here have this!" Ray thrust a bottle at me.

"Raymond! What's this—a bottle of wine?"

"Housewarming pressie," he said looking at me. "I found it in the bottle shop. Ha-ha-ha."

"What an odd place," I replied, glancing back.

"A bottle of wine—not a record?" said Margarita.

Ray laughed—like a chain saw played by a tenor recorder.

"Well come in. Wel-come-in to our humble home," I said.

"I'll open the wine. Someone will have to have a cup. Let's toss a coin, we each call, loser gets the cup."

"Do you know anything about this?" Margarita held aloft the record.

"Uh," said Ray. "Let's see—Looks like Throbbing Offal."

"You know them??" Margy said.

I splashed the red-black wine into three receptacles.

"A very strange occurrence occurred yesterday," I said.

Ray laughed.

"Here's to the new place!"

"Slàinte"

"Bottoms up!"

"Mud in your eye!"

We touched glasses, and cup, and drank.

"It's actually not funny," said Margarita. She continued:

"We're talking about it as if it's a normal thing, but what happened wasn't at all normal. It's horrific. There's been some kind of an intruder here. Yesterday we went for a walk. When we came back, this record, which neither Roxy nor I had seen before, was in here. In between my balcony-room and Roxy's room, propped up against books. Someone put it there deliberately. But there's no way that anyone could get in here!— And why this? It's really freaked us out!"

"Well, at least we think there is no way that anyone could get in," I said.

"Look! There is no way that anyone could climb from the ground, to this balcony to get in," said Margarita.

We peered out the open window, Ray in the middle.

"There's a tiny ledge on the side of the wall," I said pointing, but it's only an inch wide, and it's at least three feet from the window. I don't see how anyone could reach."

Ray poured himself another glass. I held out the cup.

"There's a gallery opening tonight, with a band playing. I thought I'd call around to see if you want to go."

"Did you know that we're all in a palindrome?"

Margarita looked at Ray.

"Eh?" said Ray.

I did a double take, and stared at her.

"Glenelg," she laughed. "Objectively speaking." He joined her in laughter.

"Actually," I said. "It was Raymond who pointed that out to me—when I lived here last year."

Margarita and I met Ray at the opening that evening, he had gone into town to his studio first and we stayed in the flat and got ready. Ray's friends were there, the Art Scandals, there were art punk bands, and it was crowded. When Margy and I were catching a cab home; Ray said that he'd had too much to drink to go home to his parents' place, and he came back to the house with us, and slept in my bed.

A few days later Ray confessed to Margy and me that he'd put the record in the flat; he said that he did climb in the window. But we didn't believe him; no one could have got in that way.

It occurred to me that maybe he knew Reggie, and he let him have the key to our room. And he didn't tell us. If so, that made it even worse.

I asked him. He laughed. "Never met him in my life!"

It remained a mystery.

A couple of days later when Margy had gone to make enquiries at the Conservatorium I left our rooms an hour or so later and caught the tram. I was wearing my black 1940s skirt and tailored top, with tennis shoes, black hat and sunglasses.

I disembarked at the Railway Station and walked into Lost Property. It was the same man behind the counter.

"Hi. I was wondering if my typewriter had been handed in?" Hope against hope. As I often said, my portable typewriter was my most precious possession.

"I think a typewriter has been handed in." He smiled.

"Oh, great!"

He returned holding a typewriter. My spirits, temporarily lifted, crashed again.

It was a cream coloured Marinetti.

I looked at it dejectedly.

"No. That's not it."

"That's not it?" He said sounding surprised.

"No, it's not. Is that the only one that's been handed in?"

"Yes," he said.

"I'll come back."

"If you leave your name, and contact details, I can make a note of it," he said.

"Roxanne Bergson. I'll come back in a few days. Thanks."

I walked out and caught the tram back to Glenelg.

A few days later, one afternoon when Ray came to visit us, we were considering what to do that night.

"I know ladies. Let's go to the Kit Kat Klub!" said Ray.

I laughed, thinking it was a joke.

"The Kit Kat Klub!' Margarita laughed too. "Yes! Let's go!"

Of course, we had never been there. It was a notorious strip joint on Hindley Street.

He said something, I was laughing, and did not quite hear.

"Tranny?" said Margarita. "You mean as in transistor radio or Rocky Horror show?"

"Yeah," he cackled. "That's it!"

"Hmm, okay," I said. It was the thing to do, I believed, to do eccentric things if you were a cutting edge artist.

We set out, as if it was a great adventure.

Margarita and I joked a bit nervously on the tram into the city centre. Ray didn't say much.

We disembarked in town and walked to the entrance of the club, on the street level.

Pink fluorescent signs proclaimed GIRLS GIRLS GIRLS and ALL NITE STRIP CLUB.

I suddenly felt a lot more apprehensive.

We walked past a couple of bouncers who looked embarrassed when they saw Margarita and me.

We followed Ray through the entrance. The beat of music shook the air. He paid and led the way. He clearly knew where to go, and must have been here before.

We passed men sitting at tables in the dark.

"Here." Ray indicated a table. I was overcome by embarrassment and mortification. Luckily it was dark. On the stage before us a woman was twirling a sequinned boa around her head, her arms covered in bruises. As she removed clothing, I was shocked to see bruises all over her body. Loud thumping disco music was playing. At the end of the performance, when all the clothes were off, she walked off stage. A master of ceremonies in tails and a top hat swaggered onto the stage.

"If anyone wants to spend time and money with Gemma upstairs, it's that way!" he gestured to a dark exit door.

"And now welcome the lovely Linda, trapeze artist *extraordinaire!* Straight from the circus!"

I was very glad the darkness hid my face from sight.

She too had bruises on her skin. All their limbs and bodies were covered in bruises. The performers all had the same glazed gaze, and looked drugged. I couldn't stand it any longer.

"Let's go. I'm going." I said loudly suddenly standing up.

Margarita jumped up. Ray didn't say anything. He followed us out.

I strode past the men on the door, furiously.

Outside Ray seemed chastened by my strong reaction.

"Shall we go to the Travellers Arms, there should be a band playing?" said Margarita.

"Okay." We went to the familiar pub, which was over the road and in a side alley.

"It's disgusting," I said as we sipped our drinks.

"All those people performing were covered in bruises. They all looked as if they were out of it; they probably have to take drugs to stand doing that work, then they get addicted."

"Working in the sex industry is a legitimate way to make money," said Margarita primly. "You're being prejudiced."

"I know someone who has worked there. She doesn't take drugs." Ray said. "It's a form of performance art."

"The art of exploitation," I said. "They all looked like they'd been beaten up. It's terrible."

It was an argument I'd had before with friends and peers. No one said they agreed, although Samuel defended my right to have this point of view. We did not talk about the place, let alone go there, again.

What was it that was out of frame? What was it that I couldn't see? In the apartment, it felt like Margy and I were travelling together in a small compartment on a train. A carriage full of uneasy energies, of transient yet stagnant forces that pulled us from side-to-side as we moved through the gloomy spaces of the big room, and balcony-room with its louvred windows and slanted floor, and back again. Drinking, eating, dressing and undressing. Talking about what we were going to do, and what we might do. My tarot deck, spread out, put away, spread out again across the big room's wooden table. Every day we read the cards. It had become a ritual between us, since we moved in, days ago.

Every time I read for her, I don't know what to say. She keeps on turning up bad omens. The hanging man, the lightning struck tower. Every day it's the same. I turn up the high priestess; the world; the lovers. One of the girls must go on a long journey of Self discovery—that is how I read the signs. But who will go, and who will stay? I see deception and betrayal in the cards. Certainties shattered... disillusion ahead. I feel sorry for Margarita as my cards are always so much better than hers. And, I cannot help but think to myself, this reflects our life in other ways.

"What do you want to do?" I ask her, staring down at the hanging man. In the dim light he is rocking, swaying gently from side to side. Upside down, a noose wrapped around his neck.

"I want to get into the Conservatorium," says Margarita. "I don't want to play electric violin. I want to go back to the violin I played when I was growing up. That I stopped when I met you."

"What do you mean, when you met me?"

"When I met you I stopped playing violin. I was 13."

"No. That was before we met, Margy. I didn't know you when you played violin. That was before we'd moved there. Remember?"

She doesn't remember. All that she mis'remembers' is that I am the catalyst of loss. The one who supposedly led her off the track. Separated her from destiny. Worse things rise up from her cards. Dark images. The fool. And the devil. Foreboding twists through my thoughts, like winding sheets.

Everything is shaking in the big room, the table with its spread deck of cards, the chairs upon which we sit, the double bed and wardrobe at the end of the bed, swaying and rocking from side to side. We gaze at the cards before us and I sense a thin, unlovely portent from the future. Rising up all around us like fumes from a swamp.

"You know, Margarita, I think you're right— think there may be dead things beneath the carpet."

Margarita could not sleep in the wall bed, she said. One night as we were preparing to get into my big bed she came into my room and asked if she could sleep in my bed with us.

I was always too generous for my own good. I just felt bad that she said she couldn't stretch her legs straight in her bed, and because of her slipped cartilage.

Next morning, she talked to Ray, but not me. She spurned me; acting towards me as if she was so angry with me she was going to petrify me with her act of icy cruelty.

I think Margarita wanted me to give her my bed. After a while I'd just about had enough. I wanted to be with him, on my own.

The Missing Typewriter

I found a new apartment for Ray and me. It had three rooms, a bedroom with bathroom ensuite, and living room connected by a kitchen; the front door opened onto the street. A back door opened off the kitchen into a yard where there was a clothesline. It was in an old building, a street back from the beach, on the opposite side of Jetty Road to Rubicon Road.

We moved in. Margy took over my room, and had enough space.

A couple of days after moving in, I returned from walking on the beach and saw a typewriter on the narrow bench table in the kitchen. It was not my lost typewriter. It was a second hand cream Marinetti like the one I'd seen at the train station Lost Property. When Ray came in, I asked him:

"Where did the typewriter come from?"

"I found it for you. I thought I'd go and ask at the train station if your typewriter had been handed in and it had so I brought it back for you."

He smiled.

"*Oh no!*" I exclaimed. "That's not my typewriter! Mine is a Giacometti. Thanks for going to check for me, but you'll have to take it back and say you made a mistake."

It was three days before Raymond was able to return the typewriter to Lost Property, and in those days everything was to radically change.

Next morning Ray woke earlier than me, and left the flat. I walked into the kitchen to make a cup of tea. The typewriter was still sitting on the bench. He had not taken it with him.

I looked at it pensively. There was some typing paper in my suitcase. My fingers were itching to write. I felt torn. I couldn't take it back because I'd already told the man in Lost Property that it wasn't mine. And that would seem odd. It had to be Raymond who took it back.

But surely it wouldn't hurt to use it while it was in the flat.

I extracted a semi-transparent sheet from the sheaf of paper in my suitcase. I sat down, inserted it top back of the roller, twisted the sidewinder and rolled it up until the clean snowy white page was facing me.

I tapped a few letters. R o x y

But it didn't feel right.

It felt as if everything had gone off skew.

I couldn't use it. It wasn't mine. Whoever had lost it was probably feeling as wretched about losing this, as I was about the loss of my typewriter.

I decided to go out for a walk along the beach. I put on my sunscreen and hat and left the flat. As I stepped onto the street I noticed a new-looking white car with black tinted windows parked opposite the front door, on the other side of the street. A man in black with dark sunglasses was sitting in the driver's seat, I saw through the windscreen; he looked up as I glanced at him curiously.

I walked down the street and into Mosley Square, past the tram stop. Squinting against the sun, I glanced up at the clock tower on the Town Hall, which faced the Bay.

3.35 p.m.

I turned left at the Regal and walked along the esplanade above the white sandy beach where children were playing, and adults basked in the autumn sunshine.

On my way back I detoured through side streets. As I was power-walking down a narrow sandy street a white car drove past. That was odd. It looked like the white car I'd seen before. Same dark tinted windows.

When I arrived back Ray was still out.

The typewriter was on the kitchen bench. It was not exactly tempting. I felt as if it was watching me. But I sat down and tapped out a few more lines.

```
visible to the seagulls, as the wind blew
and their beaks tugged at the bag covering
the dismembered body...
```

The typewriter seemed to have brought a dangerous energy into the flat and the air was crackling.

I decided to do my yoga. It was a habit, a form of exercise and meditation I had relied on since arriving in Australia and the first strange months, in University House and the house in Kambah, when I had practiced my yoga for an hour every day without fail and yoga deep breathing my entire waking days and nights. That's what kept me grounded; a fine line held my mind and body together and kept me from panicking.

I gratefully settled into the familiar stretches and poses that were comforting in the order of my routine, starting with the shoulder stand, after lying in stillness for a minute or so.

Since moving into the flat with Ray I'd been feeling more stressed. Things didn't feel quite right. Having the wrong typewriter in the flat was increasing my anxiety level. I lowered my legs from the vertical posture, over my head until my toes touched the floor; then I carefully slid my feet forwards across the floor whilst keeping my legs straight, into the Plough. I breathed deeply. In-out. In-out. I always held the pose for at least sixty deep breaths.

....38…39…40

The back door burst open.

Raymond did not come home that way. He always walked in the front door.

I froze.

"Roxy, where are you?" Margy shouted.

I'd given her a key to the back door. Reggie's Rooms was less than a ten-minute walk away. We were still able to be in close contact even though I'd moved in with Raymond, leaving her with space in the big room, and the large bed to herself so she could stretch out her legs. I was concerned about her.

"ROXY??"

She burst into the bedroom where I was immobile on the floor.

"God, I feel absolutely terrible. I don't know what's wrong, can you come over?"

"I'm doing yoga." I mumbled upside down, face squashed by the Plough, trying to block out the violent interruption into my fragile bubble of calm space.

"I have to do this. I can't stop."

"Oh Christ," she said. She paced in and out of the kitchen

and entrance to the bedroom. "Is Ray here?"

"No," I muttered.

"Well, I'll leave you to it then, Roxy!" I heard her rushing out the back door, slamming it behind her. She was obviously upset but I had to calm myself down before being able to help her.

I finished my yoga. Breathing deeply from the bottom of my lungs, I stepped into the kitchen. I couldn't seem to get away from it, the typewriter. It seemed to be looking at me, watching me. I boiled a pan of water and made camomile tea. It was almost dark, and too late to walk to Reggie's Rooms to see Margy.

I put on my yukata over my purple vest and shorts. Then I sat at the table in front of the typewriter. I wanted to write my fictional memoir about a woman who has hearing problems. But I couldn't think of what to write.

It didn't feel right. It felt like on someone else's typewriter I was typing someone else's story. There was interference on the line. Induction, cross talk, and crossed wires. Tap tap tap. Unseen threats crackled in the air.

```
The body, or what was left of it, spilled
out of the black bin bag onto the mud flat
flanking the river. Towering above it was
the bridge; they had misjudged and thrown
the bag off too far to be carried out to
sea. Instead the bag was stuck on the bank,
eddies of wind tugging at the black plastic
exposed the remains to the squawking sea
gulls and buzzing flies.
```

Where was this story coming from? A terrible crime story. It was terrifying me. That night, Raymond did not return.

Next morning, as I was tapping a few lines on the typewriter, there was a long ringing on the front door bell. Surreptitiously, I peeped through the net curtains over the kitchen window, which looked straight out onto the street outside. A large man dressed in black was standing outside the front door. I'd never seen him before. The bell rang. I jumped back from the window in case he might see there was someone behind the net.

He rang a third time, held his finger on the bell. I dropped to the floor below the level of the widow, and crawled along the lino, hiding behind the fridge. Eventually the bell stopped ringing. After the silence had lengthened, I waited for what felt like a safe length of time had elapsed before getting up. My nerves were on edge.

I needed to go out for a long walk. Walking and yoga were my major de-stressors. Sometimes writing.

As I was power walking, fast, along the Esplanade I glanced over to the road and noticed a white car with tinted windows, cruising slowly along the street next to me. Through the windscreen I could see a man in black, wearing sunglasses. It looked like he was following me down the Esplanade.

What was going on? I scrambled over the wall and jumped down onto the beach.

I took off my sandals, and walked along the edge of the sea, through the wavelets advancing and receding on the shore.

What secrets do the waves know? The waters of the Bay that the river runs into. What secrets are washed out at night under cover of dark waters...

I walked until I felt the sun stinging my face even though I was wearing sunscreen, and I turned and walked back, down to the Jetty where I climbed the steps leading from the beach to Moseley Square. In front of me, flanked by palm trees, the marble pillar of Pioneer Memorial soared into the sky, topped with the bronze replica of the sailing ship that came to shore here, in 1836. I'd read its plaques, listing the names of first explorers and settlers in South Australia. Founders on the northern side, explorers on the southern side.

As I walked further I could see on Jetty Road the flash of a white car, driven by the man in a black jacket.

The car was driving in a U-turn off Jetty Road into a side street.

I hurried into the Shopping Centre. My heart was racing. As I selected a few apples I collected my thoughts. It appeared I was being followed. By a man in a white car with black tinted windows. I felt faint with shock. I hurried to the checkout, paid for my apples, and walked out into the sunlight. I looked up and down the road, and took a deep breath of pure relief. No white cars to be seen.

I walked across Jetty Road over the tram tracks, and turned onto the Esplanade, right then left into Royalton Close. It was almost exactly parallel to 88 Rubicon Road where I'd lived last year, to the east rather than the west of Jetty Road. I walked towards the flat, opened the front door, and jumped.

Margy was standing right in front of me, looking at me.

"I was just going to open the door when I heard your key, I came around but you weren't in and I decided to stay till you got back. It's really scary at Reggie's Rooms."

"Something strange is happening," I said.

"What?"

I could see she wasn't very interested in what I was going

through because she was so concerned with her own problems. But, as I told her, her attitude changed.

"I think I'm being followed... A strange man came to the flat and rang the bell this morning... Raymond went to the railway station Lost Property to see if my typewriter had been handed in, and he brought back a typewriter that's not mine." I gestured towards it.

We looked at the typewriter, sitting on the kitchen bench, with my sheet of paper covered in typed lines in it.

"That was the day before yesterday. He's taking it back, but he hasn't been here since yesterday. He didn't say where he was going. Didn't come home last night. And I'm being followed." My voice escalated as I tried to stay calm.

"Really? Are you sure you have been? How do you know"

"Yes." I knew it sounded odd; I was trying to explain it as convincingly as I could so that she would believe me. But as I had no idea what was going on, it was hard to even say what was happening.

But she picked up on my edge of fear and we both now felt unnerved, and nervous.

"When I was walking along the esplanade yesterday a man in black driving a white car with black tinted windows was following me, I had to jump down onto the beach to get away. And then when I was walking back I saw the car at the end of Jetty Road, and a man watching me again. It started yesterday. The car was parked on the opposite side of the road outside the flat. Today, when I was walking on the esplanade, the same white car driven by a man in black was following me again. It followed me on my way as I was walking. I had to go into the shopping centre to escape it."

I started to wash the apples under the kitchen tap.

There was a rattling in the front door. Margy and I looked at each other in alarm. The door opened.

Ray walked in.

He stood in the doorway, he was carrying painting boards, and his backpack was slung over his shoulders.

"Hi," I said.

"Hello Raymond," said Margy.

"Hayoop. I'll just go and put all this stuff down." He could be heard walking down the steps into the living room, where he was setting up some of his painting things.

He walked back up into the kitchen.

"I had to sleep at the studio last night," he said to me.

"Oh." That was the last thing on my mind at the moment.

Ray made a pot of tea and we moved down into the living room area.

I was starting to tell Ray about what had been happening.

I glanced out of the living room window.

A large man dressed in a dark suit was standing at the front door.

"Oh my God, it's the same strange man who came around this morning."

The doorbell started to ring. I had a strong warning feeling, that it was dangerous.

"You go, Ray. I have no idea what's going on, but if it's for me say I'm not here."

Ray walked up the few steps from the sunken living room, to the hallway and front door; I could hear his voice, talking to the man.

After a few minutes he closed the door and came back into the living room.

"What did he want?"

"He asked if Roxanne Bergson was here."

"You're kidding."

"Come on Ray, what did he really say?"

"That's what he said. I'm not making it up."

"How could he know who I am? And where I am? Did he say who he was or what it was about?"

"No. I just said that you weren't here."

"I think it's got something to do with that typewriter. All these things happened since your brought it here Ray. Nothing like this has ever happened before. I was going to take it to the train station myself but I thought it would look odd if I took it back when I had already seen it and said that it wasn't mine. It has to be you, Ray. Something really scary is going on. I have no idea what it is."

"Hmm," he said. He stood up and emptied his backpack. We walked back up into the kitchen. I pulled out the sheet of paper covered with lines of my story, and he put the typewriter in his backpack. I glanced at the clock on the wall that Ray had put there.

"4 p.m. There's time to take it back. They close at six."

Ray laughed grimly. "Well, I'll be off then. See you on my return."

Margy and I paced around, nervously.

Ray returned about an hour and a half later.

Without the typewriter.

"How did it go?" I asked.

"It seems there is more to it than meets the eye."

"What?"

"Apparently that typewriter is connected to an international drug ring."

"*WHAT??*" I repeated.

"What do you mean?" said Margy.

"Who said that?"

"The man at Lost Property."

"What do you mean? How could he know?"

"That's all he said."

"Oh my God! And they're got my name! The man who's been following me, could he be a detective? But now the typewriter is returned, and they know it was a mistake, the wrong typewriter, it should stop it, shouldn't it?"

"I don't know," said Margy. "I'm not feeling well. All this is making me more stressed. I'm going back to the house. Do you want to walk with me?"

"Yeah, sure," I replied.

On the way to and from Reggie's Rooms, I kept glancing around. But I didn't see any white cars. I breathed more deeply just wanting to forget all about it.

That night I cuddled up to Ray. "I missed you last night," he said.

He put his arm around me and I slept deeply.

The next morning Ray left to go to his gallery in the city. I decided to go for a long walk to shake out all the cobwebs of stress and fear that I had been feeling since the wrong typewriter had entered my life. I wanted to forget about it, as if the strange, threatening and intimidating events had not happened. I decided to walk to Brighton Jetty along the beach from Glenelg, and back again. It was over ten miles there and back.

I decided to walk the first part of the way on the beach to Brighton, and half way back, then I'd climb up the wooden steps up a steep sand dune onto the road, running along above the beach, then I'd head back down to the beach.

It was a fine, clear skied Autumn day. As I walked, the sun shone on the ocean and I breathed the fresh salty air deeply as I strode fast, barefooted, along the water's edge. I walked to the Jetty, turned back and after hiking for some time, climbed the steps up the dune. As I was walking along the road, gazing out to the horizon, I heard a car engine behind me. My heart sped. A white car passed me, driving terrifyingly slowly; black tinted windows. Driven by a man in black. It parked by the side of the road, about fifty yards ahead. There were no other people, or cars, in sight. My heart raced faster with adrenalin.

What was going on? There was no way I could escape. There weren't even any houses. To my left the dunes dropped down to the beach, a sheer drop. There was a fence with strands of wire separating the top of the dunes from the road. I quickly grabbed the top and middle strands with each hand, pulling them apart, opening a space wide enough to slip through. My feet sank deeply into the soft sand as I waded through it up to my ankles, lurching forwards through the coarse tussocks to the sandy edge. It was a long way down. Taking a deep breath I launched myself off the edge, cleaving as much as possible to the sand dune, I ran, slid, rolled and tumbled all the way down, cushioned by sand. I reached the beach then jumped up and ran to the hard sand at the water's edge. I hurried all the way back.

When I walked off the beach at the Jetty, and crossed over into Moseley Square, I saw the flash of a white car in the traffic. I ducked down a side street near Royalton, my short cut to the flat. I looked around. The road was empty. I fumbled with my key and pushed it into the lock, it seemed to be blocked, the key wouldn't turn. I persisted and it unlocked.

Ray was in the living room, drawing.

"I'm still being followed," I panted. "By the man in black in the white car with tinted windows. I walked along the road at the top of the beach between Brighton and Glenelg and he passed me then stopped ahead of me on the road. I escaped by running down the sand dune."

"Hmm," he said in a serious tone. "That's well—not good." He wrinkled his brow in concern.

"Should I go to the police? Or should you go to the police and tell them?"

"No. I don't think that will work if they are following you. Not if they suspect you of being involved in this international drug ring!"

"Ha! It's ridiculous!" If it wasn't happening to me I could have laughed at the absurdity of it. But it was and I was scared.

I realized there was one thing I could do, in a dire emergency. At 7 p.m. I walked to the public phone, I nervously looked around me. I saw a white car with black windows in the distance on Jetty Road. I couldn't tell if it was the same model.

I dialled the number in my book. He answered.

"Hi Dad!"

"Oh, hello Roxanne!" His voice calm and reassuring, albeit sounding a little surprised. I never rang except on birthdays.

I told Dad about what had happened, hearing in my inner ear my words sharp with alarm.

I told him about the mix up with the typewriter and what the man at Lost Property said to Raymond about the international drug ring. Then I told Dad what I was going through:

"I'm getting really scared. I'm being followed every time I

leave the flat. By a man in black driving a white car with black tinted windows. I might have been followed to the phone box now. In the daytime, ever since Raymond brought the wrong typewriter back, I've been followed by the man in a white car with black windows. I was followed today when I was walking by the beach on the road. I ran down a sand dune to get away. I was scared. And I saw a white car with black windows on the way here to the phone."

Dad took it very seriously.

"Is there anything that you know of that could have given rise to this, Roxanne?" His voice was grave.

"No! I hate drugs. I never take them."

Then I remembered.

"Last year, in the house I was living in, one of the students who lived there, Fraser, made up lies to the police that I took drugs, and police officers came and searched my room."

"*What?*" said Dad.

"Yes. Of course, they didn't find anything. I've never taken drugs. The police officers searched my room, and then left. I didn't hear anything about it afterwards. It was awful. He was aggressive and paranoid. That's all I can think of."

"Really?" He sounded shocked, and a bit angry.

"Yes." I had not thought about it since, until now. So many things happened, and I just carried on with my life.

Dad was always a rock of calm rationality in an emergency.

"I will ring the Detective Chief Superintendent tomorrow, and tell him what has been happening, and that there's been a mistake about the typewriter."

"Will that be enough to stop it?"

"Yes. Of course. If anything else happens let me know."

Rocky Horror Show

Hey, do you guys want to go and see the Rocky Horror Show? Margarita asked. Ray and I had run into her, by chance, at a mid-day opening at the Photographer's Gallery in the city. It was over three months since I'd moved out of Reggie's Room. After the holiday flat in Royalton Road, Ray and I had recently moved to Brighton. I'd wanted to get away from Glenelg, and start again in a new place. Brighton was still not far away, but it was better.

Ray and I had driven into the city, to look at the new Art Scandals studio. There was a large crowd at the opening.

"I've never seen it," Margarita continued. "But it should be good fun. Lots of people get dressed up. It's on in the old art cinema. "

"Yeah, it's been running for years," said Ray. "Yeah, sure we'll go, sport."

I was astonished, but if he wanted to, that was cool by me. We arranged to pick up Margarita, at Reggie's Rooms, in our new car.

I'd bought the car although I couldn't drive. It was a vintage model. Ray and I had walked past it parked in a side street and

Ray saw the *For Sale $500* notice on its windscreen. I love those cars, he said. I looked at it with new interest. I went back alone, wrote down the phone number on the notice, and said, if there were nothing wrong with it, I'd buy it, for him. I wanted to give Ray what he wanted. One day, Ray and I had done the beach walk from Glenelg, when after more than an hour's walking along the sand, we'd reached Brighton Jetty, he'd pointed to the tall weatherboard building that rose three storeys high above a bait and tackle shop, opposite the pier.

"I've always wanted to live there," he said.

"Do you still want us to get a place on our own together?"

"Okay," he replied.

Next day, I had walked there on my own. I went into the bait and tackle shop, and asked the elderly hunched woman behind the counter, if there were any empty flats.

"Yes," she'd said. Looking at me closely with black, appraising eyes. "Third floor."

The third floor! I followed her up the staircase to the flat. A bedroom, a kitchen, a bathroom, living room, and a glassed-in balcony, facing the sea...I gazed out into infinite space, radiant light. It was like looking into eternity, *sea merging with the sky*, the materialisation of a poem by Rimbaud.

Without delay, I went to the local ATM, withdrew money for the deposit and hurried back to the shop to give it to my new landlady.

I wanted to be on my own with Ray, the two of us, isolated from the world, living in our own private realm of light, like it had been in the first days we spent together.

We'd been living alone together in our new flat and hardly saw

Margy these days. When we ran into her at the opening she was very worried. She said that the previous night when she returned from the Conservatorium, there'd been a drunken man slumped in the doorway to her apartment.

I was sipping a glass of red wine, looking at a silver gelatin photographic print of reflections of a lighthouse in pools of water. I wasn't paying much attention to what she was saying, as she was addressing her story to Ray. I was pretending that I hadn't noticed that, once again, she preferred to talk to him, rather than me.

"I wasn't sure if he was asleep or not." In spite of myself I found myself listening.

"He was holding a bottle. It was dark as I came up the stairs and almost didn't see him, and then suddenly I did. It gave me a terrible shock. I almost dropped my violin on him…"

My partner was looking at her very seriously; his eyes fixed behind his glasses, nodding his head in sympathy. Why was she telling him, not me? I didn't say anything, and went to get another refill from the drinks table.

Late the next night, after the three of us went to see the Rocky Horror Show in the wooden theatre, surrounded by dozens of screaming suburbanites in lingerie and gothic make-up, we drove Margarita home. We stopped on the unlit street outside the house that loomed high against the dark night. Margarita stepped out of the car and closed the door.

Then Margy stooped down to Ray's window on the driver's side, as though a thought had just occurred to her.

"I say, would either of you two kind chaps care to walk me up to my door?" she asked in the exaggerated English upper-class accent, one of the voices that we used to put on to amuse ourselves, in our younger days. It didn't cover up the anxiety that showed in her eyes and nervous smile, doubly nervous, for asking us.

"Go up by yourself, you chicken-livered coward," I replied with an Aussie twang. I was joking, my hand was on the door handle, pushing it down, to get out and go up with her.

But before I could do that, Ray swung around, with a look of fury on his face.

"I'll go up with her," he said. For a moment I was shocked. Until I realized he couldn't really be angry, he was only joking, putting it on, like Margarita putting on her fear, and English accent; and me putting on an exaggerated Australian accent. He jumped out, slamming the door. I watched them walk up the flight of steps to the house, which towered like a haunted castle filled with drifting ghosts. Ray behind Margarita, who, in the confusion, hadn't remembered to say good-bye, but that didn't perturb me; I knew that she knew that I was joking. She'd be laughing now.

I was still smiling as he returned to the car. He was joking too, I knew. I'd never known him get angry. He opened the door and sat in the deep red upholstered driver's seat. All his movements were taut with white-lipped controlled fury.

I turned to him with a smile, "I was only jo—" I started to say, but my words were cut off as he accelerated off down the street, driving furiously. His eyes lasered the road ahead. Lips set tight in a white mask of rage. He couldn't be serious. What was wrong with him?

He was driving fast, too fast. I glanced at the speedometer. It was quivering at the upper limit, admittedly that might not be too dangerous in itself, not in that car. But Ray's mood was making me nervous. We were driving along the long straight flat stretch of road that ran parallel to the beach, and the sand dunes, approaching the railway crossing.

"Slow down, Ray," I put a steadying hand onto his arm. He shook my hand off and lashed out at me verbally,

"Just shut up, who do you think you are?"

There was not much I could say to that. It was not so much the rhetorical question as his body language, the rigid bars of his arms, whiteness of his knuckles, his hands gripping the steering wheel. He looked like a furious maniac impersonation. I had an overwhelming urge to burst out laughing; but I managed to stop myself just in time.

He was mad when we got out of the car. He was mad as we climbed the staircase to our apartment. He was still mad, seething, as he turned the key in the front door and we walked in, and he ignored me and went into the kitchen. As I cleaned my teeth and got into bed, I could hear him, he was stamping, moving things, and muttering to himself, in the space where he worked. Or, rather, where he'd been trying to work, in the living room section that connected the kitchen and bathroom with the balcony room.

Ever since summer, when he failed to start his conceptual masterpiece in his shack in the rainforest, the brilliant work of genius locked away in his head, he'd continued to try. Started dozens of times. Done countless drawings and thrown away most of those I'd seen...

He reminded me of Margarita with her unfinished fugue. Whereas she was obsessed with trying to find a perfect ending, he was searching to find a perfect beginning for his work; the breakthrough-concept from which a work of genius will grow, and nothing else will do.

And now it sounded like he'd lost it. Lost his temper, lost his mind. "Lose your temper and you're a loser," I was tempted to shout through the bedroom door. I was shocked and irritated that he was imposing his dark mood in our home. But I kept my thoughts to myself. It was safer that way.

I tried to focus on the sounds of the waves breaking onto the sand, as the street-light flickered beneath the window, in the night of long knives, forks and spoons, rattling in the kitchen. And as he paced, in and out of the kitchen, bathroom, balcony, living room, stamping and talking to himself, all through the night—why was he shaking the cutlery drawer? What was he getting out?—I lay shivering in fear between cold sheets.

"I'm going to visit Margarita," said Ray, early one morning a couple of days later. He was walking into the balcony-room where I was writing. I noticed that he was holding a bottle of red wine; with a flamboyant flourish he slid the wine into his knapsack; his manner seemed defiant. I was amused, in a detached way. I wasn't worried that he wanted to visit my friend.

No, I thought. It was good that at least one of us was going to visit her. I would rather it were he, as I was busy. I didn't feel guilty that Margarita was alone in Reggie's Rooms. She was studying at the Conservatorium, which was taking up her time. She was doing what she wanted. We were both twenty-one. We needed to forge our separate lives. She was sure to find a boyfriend of her own soon.

With Ray gone, it just meant that I would have the flat to myself, my crystal prism of light. A few more hours absorbed in the river-rush of thoughts and dreams I was working into my intricately patterned 'states of mind—inner peace' series. I looked at him calmly, filled with tranquillity and said—"don't you know I like to be alone, to paint?"

He opened the front door. "You should eat something," he said disapprovingly.

"Okay, Dad," I replied. He looked at me with his white, blanked-out expression, and closed the door behind him.

I was fasting to achieve inner peace. It was two days since I'd eaten anything. Never before had I felt such a sense of light ecstatic transcendence. I was fasting to paint powerfully and essentially. I was fasting for my art. By leaving me alone, Ray was doing me a favour…

But the sharpness in his voice, the disapproving quality of his final words to me, the look of displeasure on his face, were edges of unpleasantness that I was trying to ignore, as I paced around the flat.

I looked down at the beach, and watched my love walking away. A determined figure dressed in blue shorts, blue tee-shirt, straw hat; canvas knapsack on his back. He strode along the sand, double line of footprints vanishing behind him. He reached the tall white dune, where the beach curved, and disappeared. I was, in that overall time, attempting the impossible, trying to paint music. Not painting to music, but letting hand and mind go, in a coordinated dance, and painting the feeling and vibrations of the sounds in symbols of intuitive invention and fluid colour forms that flowed from my brush in time to the music I listened to. I painted in watercolour.

I was also writing a fictional memoir, by a woman living alone in a caravan by the sea whose only contact with other people is listening to radio broadcasts in foreign languages she doesn't understand. That day, I kept going around in circles. I didn't try to paint. I couldn't concentrate on abstract language works now, or dream-pieces.

At the end of the glassed-in balcony, Ray had stored some things. He had talked about working here, setting up a desk to work on ideas in visual notebooks. But that was before I'd moved my table in, and taken up almost permanent residence.

At the beginning of the semester, I had decided to postpone my course. I decided that a better use of my time was living with Ray and developing my own painting and writing styles, in our shared prism of light.

Forest Floor #3 (Sprite)

There were piles of his things lying around. Folios, visual diaries, canvases, propped against the wall, stacks of books on the floor.

I stood up; paced around. Couldn't concentrate. I wandered into 'his' side of the balcony-room. I felt that it was a touch illicit, my being in 'his' space. On his table were his precious prisms. I picked one up. Held it high, behold, the pure light of sea and sky. I watched the rainbows revealed, sliding across the sharply angled planes, through the shining glassy surfaces.

A few tapes were on his table with his cassette player. I put on Joy Division, *Unknown Pleasures*. The brilliant light, dark emotion; I felt as if I could lose myself in this music. I picked up one of Ray's folders of work...

Again, there were a couple of pages of contact sheets.

I stared at the images in sudden revulsion. Ray's face was covered in slashes, blood oozing out of them, he was cutting his cheeks, his forehead, chin; his eyes were glassy, he looked unwell...ill. Just looking at this work, by myself, without him or anyone else there to explain it, provoked a natural response. I saw his images of self-mutilation as outward and confronting signs of disturbing inner conditions, and not, as some people talked of them, as a cool indicator of the cutting-edge quality of his art.

I turned to what was underneath:

A large black and white print, three people sitting at a café table. Ray was in-between a man and a woman I'd never seen before. She was beautiful, sensual, with dark wavy hair, hoop earrings, she looked like a gypsy, her low-cut dress revealing cleavage. The man beside her was muscular, swarthy, wearing a film-gangster-style suit. Ray's eyes were huge, glazed, as he stared at the camera with a strange, creepily enigmatic smile. Like an underworld pin-up boy. He'd talked about his "sedative-phase." Was this part of it? Was this theatre, or 'real' life? What disturbing drama lay beneath the scenario in this image?

I jumped as I turned to the next photograph.

Who was that? I gazed at the face of a smiling man made up with red lipstick, eyeliner, blue eye shadow, mascara, eyebrows drawn on with pencil, full theatrical make up.

Made up, but discernibly male as shown by the size of nose, and heavyset jaw and chin.

I turned it over. Handwritten, on the back in a large elegant script in ink pen, were the words:

To Ray Doe love from George.

My heart leapt, my legs started trembling weakly. This was George?

Was it performance art? I had never seen this person before I was sure. Who was he or she?

I recoiled from the image, from all the images.

This wasn't the Ray I knew. But who was? And who were these friends or associates whom I had never met?

I felt shocked, frightened.

It was like looking at a stranger. And suddenly it occurred to me that I really didn't know Raymond Furnett, and his life, at all.

Ray arrived back the next afternoon. He said that he had slept in the new studio, in town.

I wanted to talk to Margy about Ray. One evening I walked there. Five miles (eight k's) through the dark streets. I walked up the boarding house stairs. Floating in the dark air, I could hear the fugue I'd heard before. I knocked on her door, loudly.

"Margy," I called out. "It's me. Let me in."

But she wouldn't open the door.

I walked there again the next night. I had to speak to her. It was mid-winter, a cold, dark evening. I'd walked from Brighton, through the back streets, not trusting the beach. I stomped up the old staircase, over the threadbare carpet, under the dim low-wattage light bulb, hanging from the ceiling. Rapped my knuckles loudly on the familiar white chipboard door.

"Who is IT?"

"It's me. I have to talk Margy, it's urgent."

"I'm not going out."

"I just want to talk."

"I don't want to talk."

"Why not? What's wrong with you?"

"Because I'm busy and I have to get up early."

"Well at least open the door."

"No— I'm not going to Roxy."

"Would you damn well open the door?" I shouted. I knew it was the only way to get her to.

"Keep your voice down, how dare you swear and shout like that?" Margy said furiously through the wood.

"I'm going to keep on shouting until you do."

She was glaring at me as she opened the door.

"Let's go to the Italian café on the main street, let's go and have a coffee. I've got to talk to you."

She was looking at me as if she hated me.

"Margy, come on. I'm not going to go away until we talk."

"All right, but I'm only going to stay out for a few minutes," she snapped, defensively. I knew it would be impossible to talk in the flat, after everything that had, and hadn't, happened in my old room.

The Italian café was almost empty. The tired, middle-aged male proprietor looked at us warily from behind the counter, and yawned. The machine hissed. He placed the cappuccinos before us; they steamed desolately.

Margarita's expression was cold, disdainful, closed. She had a haughty look that didn't suit her.

"Something's wrong with Ray," I said.

She looked at me warily.

I continued, confiding in her, as in the old times.

"He's acting really strange. Every night he stays up. I hear him as I lie awake in bed. I hear him prowling around the flat; I hear him talking. I hear him hitting walls, banging things, shouting. I hear him walking around in the kitchen; I hear the cutlery rattling as if he's getting a knife. I'm terrified that he is, and that he's coming in to knife me! I'm too scared to move..."

She made a snorting sound, and was looking at me with an expression of derision, as if there was something wrong with me, and she was still angry with me.

I said, trying again, "It's been like this since the night we went to see the Rocky Horror Show. He's stayed up all night, pacing the flat, talking and muttering to himself. 'Working on his painting.' His breakthrough piece, "Boy Ray wrestles with the angel of light," as he puts it; he thinks it will be the work that concretely proves truths that alchemists searched for, the philosopher's stone in paint. He says he's trying to find, in his mind, something he can put into his art, which will transform the way people see colour and line... Some nights he stays over at the new studio all night, working."

She snorted cynically, still looking like she thought I was the one who was overstepping boundaries.

"I think it's starting to drive him mad, driving him crazy. Angel of light, devil of darkness, it seems with him, one cannot exist without the other. I'm scared Margarita. I actually am. Scared...of him."

"I've got to go. I need to get to bed." She avoided my eyes; whipped out her purse, and jumped up to pay for her coffee.

"There's something else I haven't told you."

She paused and waited for my words.

"I think he might be having an affair with a transvestite!"

"For God's sake," she snapped, "What's wrong with you?" She stalked to the counter, paid quickly and left.

On the table was a newspaper. My gaze was drawn to the headline.

THE BROTHERHOOD SUSPECTED OF LINKS TO YOUTH MURDERS

In a radio interview concerning the murder of an as yet unidentified teenage youth, today a police detective referred to an alleged homosexual ring of prominent unidentified figures in the church and high society, as "the Brotherhood." A ring of unidentified high profile businessmen, churchmen, and physicians is allegedly connected to the recent abductions, and horrific ritual murders of teenage boys and men. Amongst the victims are several youths who were in religious and State institutions, as well as teenagers from the 'alternative' counter culture. The alleged group includes descendants of WW2 war criminals, and fascists, whose trials are pending.

Churchmen? High society? Murders? How could this be true?
I turned the page quickly.

MURDERED YOUTH BEARS MARKS OF "BROTHERHOOD" KILLING

The Brotherhood Kills Again?

Police are calling on the public for any information about the identity of the young male, whose mutilated body was found wrapped in garbage bags in a gas powered refrigerator at a fairy-floss stall at Glenelg funfair last Sunday night. Alleged cause of death is said to be severe loss of blood from an injury, which is consistent with the barbaric killing of the four youths, linked to the group of alleged suspects known as "the Brotherhood".

The café tilted sideways. I gripped onto the edge of the table until my balance returned. What was going on here? This was why I did not read the newspapers. I felt faint.

Maybe I needed to eat something. I'd forgotten. This was the result of low blood sugar caused by shock. And vasovagal syndrome.

I stood up unsteadily, and lurched to the counter.

"A piece of vegetarian pizza, and chocolate cake, and a cappuccino, please."

I wolfed the food down. Sipped the coffee gratefully.

Outside the window was Jetty Road. The silent tramlines. Above the shuttered-up shops the sky was black. I could just see the top of the Big Wheel above the supermarket roof.

I paid for my meal. Caught a late bus back to the new flat. Ray returned later.

That night I lay in bed. Terrified. It must have been after 3 a.m. The bedroom flickered, lit by the sodium glow of the broken street light outside the window. The half-light, the endless melancholy ocean sounds, restlessly, eternally eroding the shoreline. It felt like the longest night of my life. Earlier I had called him into the room.

"Ray—are you coming to bed?"

He swung in through the bedroom door, asserting angular menace and no-good testosterone. Sat on the edge of the bed, fists clenched.

"Am I coming to bed? You think you have the right to say that do you?? Do you, do you??" He shouted. I laughed, or tried to, still not fully believing he was for real.

"It's funny is it? I'm funny am I? Am I?" He towered above me.

"Why do you want me—to come—to bed? What right do you have, to say what to do? Some people have to work you know, some people are trying to do something... You wouldn't know that, would you?" He jabbed my forearm with his sharp finger.

"You don't know what it's like to really work. What have you ever done?"

Then he jumped off the bed, and stalked out. The muttering and the rattling and the prowling began again.

I'd had enough. I had to leave. Flee. Before it was too late. If I stayed, I knew my life would be in danger.

A crazy stranger had taken over. The Ray I thought I knew, the Ray I'd fallen for, had disappeared. Where was he? I had mistaken his mathematical quest for misunderstood genius. I had thought that maybe the drugs, drinking, were the dark shadow of his brilliant talent. The darkness in which the seeds of his creativity grew... Now I thought that he was disturbed, ill.

I had to go. Put some distance between us. Again. I was confused. Once more, I had to be alone.

Two days later, I'd bought my ticket; and was packing my bags, ready to leave that evening. He walked into the kitchen, a look of disbelief on his face.

"You don't mean it, you're not really going?" Unguarded as a child, his face was almost crumpling, on the verge of tears. But my mind was made up. "Of course I'm going. I said I was, didn't I?"

I walked into the bathroom to pack up my toiletries bag.

It felt good to turn the tables on him and give him a taste of his own medicine for a short while but the grand gesture backfired. As soon as I had left, on the way to Canberra, the memories started to haunt me; my mind kept replaying my last view of them. Ray, in his white cotton trousers and blue sweater, standing with Margarita in her 1940's navy dress and ankle boots, side by side on the platform, waving me off in the departing train that was gathering speed by the second.

The after-image of Ray and his waving fingers, white hand, white face, shock of red hair, bemused expression; beside him, Margarita. Until the train carried me onwards, and the two of them were lost to sight.

Departure
1982

I arrived back in Canberra in late June. I had planned to stay at the Farm for a while, although I hadn't worked out the logistics of how I'd get there. When I arrived back at Mum's place, Alex said Samuel had returned to Canberra from Israel the week before. "He's going to go down to the Farm," Alex said.

"What do you mean, how can he?"

"He asked Mum and she said he could."

It was strange. Now that I was no longer in a relationship with Samuel, several in the family who'd been so against him when I was with him seemed finally to have accepted him.

Mum wasn't pleased with me for 'dropping out' as she put it.

"I haven't dropped out, I've deferred indefinitely," I said. "I can return to finish my degree within the next ten years. And I plan to do that."

As we had both planned to go the Farm, Samuel and I went together, on his motorbike. "Like old times," he said. It was cold; it snowed more than I had ever seen there. We barricaded ourselves in the farmhouse; hardly moving from in front of the fire in the fireplace, except to chop logs in the blizzard outside, for the living room fire, and to cook lentil and vegetable stews in the cast iron pot on the wood-burning stove in the kitchen.

Samuel told me something terrible. That he'd been told by friends from school when he arrived back. One of the girls in my year, a friend, had been murdered, when she was hitching.

"Loretta was hitching from Canberra to Sydney in a truck. Bastard murdered her with an axe. They haven't caught him."

"Oh my God." I started to cry.

At night, in front of the fire I was crocheting, making a bag. The feeling of the wool and rhythm of the crochet hook were reassuring. It was a long while since I had crocheted.

"Stay here," said Samuel. "You can transfer your studies to Sydney University, we can move to Sydney!"

"I can't Samuel," I said, "I have to go away, for a while."

When Samuel and I had first been drawn together at a full moon dance beside the Lake in Canberra, I thought that I might go out with him for a couple of weeks, no more. My parents' overreaction to my starting to go out with him had the effect of thrusting me into a de facto relationship that lasted four years, from when I was seventeen, and he nineteen. Samuel was my security in those times. He protected me, a bodyguard, loyal (albeit not as faithful as I had wished) but despite his admirable qualities that I loved (and I did love him), I couldn't run the risk of staying with him; and now, when I had the chance, of going back to him.

Most of the time I lived with him I had health problems, amenorrhoea (I had a test, doctors suspected I had a pituitary gland problem, tests showed I didn't), indigestion, heartburn, though I didn't eat much, and red lesions. Doctors said these were symptoms of suppressed anxiety and stress (which, indirectly, the parents made me feel). When I had left Samuel, it all regulated, and the indigestion, and chilblains, disappeared. It shows the deep ways others can affect us, even when we think we are resisting their influence.

I had savings left over from working as a waitress before we travelled around Australia. I decided to go to Italy. I wanted to visit Baroque cathedrals and churches. I'd heard about villages in the hills of Umbria and Tuscany, where art works by Caravaggio and Michelangelo could be found in humble corners of local churches.

I would collect myself in Italy and then return to Adelaide, to Ray. Waiting for something that you think you want only intensifies the pleasure of gratification when you finally do fulfil your desire.

After staying four weeks at the Farm, Samuel and I returned to Canberra. I booked a return plane ticket. I had decided to visit sister Lily first. I sent Margy, and Ray, post-cards to say that I was going to Europe for three weeks. I thought it important. To show I wasn't dependent on them.

Margy rang to say she was coming to Sydney to see me off.

I told her about Loretta. It was hard to say anything. It was gazing into the abyss.

She arrived at the house in Canberra, a week or so later, the day before my flight.

I was very glad to see her, and appreciated her visit, but for some reason I couldn't say that to her directly.

On the evening she arrived she was excited, restless, laughing.

Hyperactive, I thought in irritation, as I dried my hair with the blow-drier in the kitchen. She kept prancing around the kitchen as if she was on speed, which sometimes she took.

Eventually she said, "I've got something to tell you."

"What?" I asked distantly.

"You must be able to guess," she teased.

"What are you talking about?" I wasn't in the mood for games.

"You must surely know what I'm going to say..."

"No, I don't, Margy," I said. I was thinking about Michelangelo's David—the fineness of his torso and legs and surprising downward slope of the shoulders. It puzzled me that he was supposed to be the epitome of male beauty...No doubt I was distracting myself with trivia.

"Come on, Roxy-baby, you do know," she interrupted my thoughts.

"No."

"Oh come on, don't tease me Roxy!"

"_"

"You do know, don't you, of course you know?"

"__"

"You have to know. It's obvious!!"

"---"

"I mean what else could happen, if you really think about it?"

"For goodness sake, Margy, I have no idea what you're on about," I muttered, brushing my hair.

"I've moved into your apartment," she said.

"Raymond and I are having a relationship!"

I placed the hairbrush carefully on the bench. I couldn't say anything. I walked out the room.

I changed my flight to one way. I vowed to myself that I would never return while they were together. I bid goodbye to Margy in Mum's garden, my voice crackling, and echoing in my ears like the static of a long-distance phone call. I couldn't look at her.

"Be careful in Adelaide," I said.

"Of course," she replied.

We stood, looking at each other; he took out a wad of notes from his pocket.

"Here," he put the bundle of the bank notes into the front pocket of my jeans.

"Oh Samuel, no—please, I don't want your money."

"What if you want to come back?" His eyes were glittering. "You'll need money for your ticket back."

"Oh, okay then," I squeezed his hand.

"I'm going to miss you Roxy," he said, tears in his eyes.

"I'll miss you, too," I replied. We looked at each other, and he held onto my hands tightly.

"You know you don't have to go, you can stay—Roxy, why don't you stay," he said.

"I've got to go," I said, squeezing his hand. "Or I'll miss my flight. Sayonara, baby."

It felt like an anti-climax. I had expected that I might feel upset to be leaving or nervous about flying.

But I felt nothing.

As the plane was flying over the South China Sea, the words of the dream puzzle returned to me.

> Cross the Rubicon
> and you will see
> a darker entrance
> to the sea
>
> a funfair waits
> on the other side
> you don't see the horror
> till you go on the ride
>
> a creepy clown C
> repeats D to infinity
> you're on the way
> when she says 'Gee'

Much later than when I first wrote it down I realized what this dream riddle, or puzzle canon, meant.

Understood musically the letters stood for the names of the notes of the keys of the fugues Margy played.

Ray's alter ego was

D or Doe- a Fugue in D

Ending it all was G for George. A Fugue in G

Ray was what in this mystery; a red handed herring? not to gild the lily—but what about D?

Crossing the Rubicon was the road. A body was found in the

funfair. The creepy clown 'C' could have been Carl, or Ray in his clown face alter ego repeating 'D' (Doe) to infinity in the hall of mirrors. It started with Margarita ('gee') but it was G. George, who ended it all.

That was nothing compared to what actually happened, the real murders, whose horror eclipses this murder metaphor for betrayal, and the loss of self and others. The self that one is in relationships with significant others, in which one becomes a uniquely different variation of oneself. I was one of the lucky ones. I got away.

Slugs

Clogging the gutters
a bulbous fraternity of slugs
has gathered
to cross silvery trails
in dusk's half light.
With fat grey skirts
orange-hemmed
they roll up like tongues,
sticky at the root.

As children
we religiously ripped apart
the squalid conventions
fascinated by our victims' pain
we saw their gaping fluted wounds
as ugly breathing flowers,
squeezed obscene lips
from the pouting fleshy petals
kissing and sucking
at the empty air
between our fingers.
We were not ashamed.

Now i try to forget—
but they insidiously
drag towards me,
smearing through my mind
with the terrible tearing sound
of glutinous resisting flesh.
Passing beneath the gutter
i am repulsed, sickened,
but cannot stay away...

Winter is damp here,
my hidden family thrives.
At night, alone
i hear the rain,
gutters gurgle, overflow—
wash out forboding
with childhood dreams...

Nicky was always leader.
I wanted us to marry,
but he said No—he was going
to join the army.

One day
out slugging, needle-armed, alert
his bold boy's bravado set new rules—
With clean pink mouth opened wide
he bit his speared slug in two,
swallowed the large mouthful whole
then, laughing, passed the rest to me.

Severed, palpitating,
the clammy body
oozed thick yellowish fluids—
my stomach churned, weakened, scared.
Despite his taunts and jeers
i could not put
that foul bleeding thing
between my lips.

But i'm older now—
i have years of courage.
Nicky—you didn't become a soldier,

instead you're at Cambridge
reading ancient history.
And we're still not married.

Patiently i await spring.
My bridal brood
will be so succulent
after winter's ritualistic rains.

Meanwhile i sharpen
my teeth on bone,
stuff bottom drawers
full with rotting tongues.

RUTH SKILBECK, 1980

Notes

Heatwave

1. p. 98. Roxy is thinking of Samuel Taylor Coleridge's poem 'The Rime of the Ancyent Marinere' (in *Lyrical Ballads with a Few Other Poems* by William Wordsworth and Samuel Taylor Coleridge, first published in 1798*)* and the lines: "As idle as a painted ship/ Upon a painted ocean."

Rocky Horror Show

2. p 215. Roxy quotes from Arthur Rimbaud's lines in *Les Illuminations* (Illuminations) 'Éternité' (Eternity) (1872-1873) also in *Une saison en enfer* (A Season in Hell) 'Faim' (Hunger) (1873) in *Oeuvres de Arthur Rimbaud: Vers et proses: Revues sur les manuscrits originaux et les premières éditions mises en ordre et annotées par Paterne Berrichon; poèmes retrouvés* (1921). Translation by Ruth Skilbeck.

p. 221. Photograph by Ruth Skilbeck: *Forest Floor #3 (Sprite)*, 2019.

Acknowledgement

'Slugs' was published in *LiNQ (Literature in North Queensland)* Vol. 8 No. 1 (1980) pp 71-72

Author's Note

The novel is set in Australia in 1980-1982. In this context the references to murders in the fictional story are fictional. They may be read as based on the actual murders in Australia, and Adelaide, in the 1970s and 1980s referred to in the news media as the 'Family murders,' the 'hitchhiker murders', and also to the disappearance of the Beaumont children in 1966, from Glenelg Beach, widely reported in the media. In my research I read news reports and articles about some of the murders and disappearances, however the novel is a work of fiction, the details in reference to 'news' in conversations, and news articles and headlines written in the novel are fictional, the characters and their stories are fictional and no reference whatsoever to any actual person, living or dead, is implied or intended. The murders and other events are included in relation to the fictional stories of the characters, to create a realistic background setting. The poem *Slugs* is symbolic, I see now, a metaphor and a pun on the term 'biting the bullet' ('slug') or having courage.

About the Author

Ruth Skilbeck is the author of books of fiction and non-fiction including new editions of novels in her Australian Fugue Series, *The Antipode Room* (2023) and *Sayonara Baby* (2023); and musico-literary studies book *The Writer's Fugue: Musicalization, Trauma and Subjectivity in the Literature of Modernity* (2016; 2017). After a career as a freelance journalist in Dublin, London and Sydney that included founding a media arts writing business; and later on teaching journalism writing (feature writing and writing for media) at the University of New South Wales; she founded a publishing house Postmistress Press, later Borderstream Books, and *Arts Features International* journal, as editor-in-chief, contributing writer, and arts photographer.